Learning To Hotwife

By Vickie Vaughan

When a male exchange student walks out of the airport to stay with them for six weeks, Gabrielle doesn't think it's a big deal, even though they thought he was a she. After all, she and her husband Jack need the money. That is, until she hears the Latino stud seducing a woman and sees the size of what he's got under his clothes. Massive.

Under her very roof while Jack is away constantly, is a young stud she can't stop fantasizing about. And when the opportunity comes to watch him in action, she can't resist. There's no way to stop herself craving seduction of the young student right across the hallway. Obsession with his size brings her to the peak of craving another man.

One night, things go over the edge, and it means Gabrielle is not only the object of two men's affection, she wants her husband to join with her hot fantasy of their young man claiming her with his exceptional sexual prowess.

Will Jack accept it? Allow her to indulge her fantasy of experiencing the biggest man she's ever had – while he watches?

If you are interested in your own custom erotic story, I am available on Fiverr:

https://www.fiverr.com/share/5K9Q4Q

Find me on Twitter: @vickieverotica

Find me on my website: www.vickievaughan.ca

Join my newsletter and receive promotions and free beta copies of upcoming books!

I genuinely love my readers and hope that we can connect! It's been a while since I've been able to publish, so please let me know if you enjoyed this story by leaving a review where you found it!

CHAPTER ONE

ﾍe airport was bustling as usual. Seeing all the travelers coming through the gates ﾍoking tanned and relaxed made Gabrielle jealous. It had been a couple of years since ﾍe and her husband Jack had gone on a vacation, which was precisely why they were ﾍanding in an airport waiting for someone.

ﾍith the economy the way it was, Jack was traveling more than ever for work, but they ﾍll had a hard time finding extra money, so a couple of years before had begun to take ﾍ students for six-week courses.

ﾍey would come from other countries, stay in an English-speaking place for some time ﾍd then head back, and the agency and school would pay the couple a decent amount ﾍt to house and feed them. Plus, in theory, keep them out of trouble. That extra money ﾍowed them to upgrade their holiday accommodations once a year, so it was worth it.

ﾍck was standing in front of her with a sign reading *Jordan*. The student was coming ﾍm Argentina and was supposed to know some English and Spanish as well. Gabrielle ﾍways wanted people from her old country, even though she was originally from ﾍother part of South America.

ﾍhen she went away to school, her family had saved up a lot of money to send her to ﾍe United States, and the rest was history. She had a decent part-time career working ﾍ PR, had met Jack right out of university and had settled down like any other ﾍmigrant to the country.

ﾍ steady flood of people was coming out of the baggage claim area, and some of the ﾍunger ones caught her eye as she waited. Young students, so full of energy and life. ﾍwas nice sometimes to hear their stories and get to know other sides of the world. A ﾍuple of their students had even returned to the US just like she did. The land of ﾍportunity, or so they said. It had been for her, that was for sure.

ﾍe tall boy caught her eye as he wheeled his suitcase out easily. Dressed in the ﾍpical Latin style, he wore a rakish grey hat and skinny jeans, almost molded to his ﾍhletic frame. He was tall and lean and had that twinkle in his eyes of a man who could ﾍsically flirt his way into whatever he wanted.

ﾍabrielle had known a ton of guys who acted like that, especially from her home ﾍuntry. This one, however, walked up to Jack and greeted him with an even wider grin.

ﾍou are the Richards? *Mi amo es Jordi.*" The boy said. Jack looked confused.

ﾍrdi? You are…Jordan?" Jack said.

ﾍ nodded. "*Si.* But you can call me Jordi. I am here to meet you?" Jack looked at ﾍabrielle and widened his eyes.

They had specifically requested a female student, and when the response came from the school, the name implied it was likely to be a girl. But the male student standing in front of them with a big grin was definitely their person. He stood there expectantly. "Is…*un problema?*"

Gabrielle was a bit taken aback. It would be the first time they would have a male student living with them, and while it really shouldn't have been a big deal, she didn't know how she felt about another man sharing their home. Girls were easy and usually kept to themselves.

She'd read stories on the company message boards about male students getting into sorts of mischief, taking advantage of the fact they were in another country. But that didn't mean she should judge Jordi before they got to know the situation.

Jack seemed to be nonplussed about the situation. After all, they were still getting the money for the student regardless, and for six weeks of food and having him around, it was enough to pay for the two of them to go away afterwards for a nice trip. "*Mucho gusto, Jordi.*" He grabbed the suitcase. "How much English do you know?"

"I know…a but?" the young man offered.

Gabrielle laughed. "A *bit*. It means a little amount. *Yo soy de Ecuador.*" Jordi's face lit up.

"Ah! *Fantastico!*" It was always easier for Gabrielle to be a bit of a go-between from the students to Jack, although he had picked up quite a bit of Spanish from their students and also when he was trying to woo Gabrielle. She'd been impressed with how quickly he picked it up, but since he never really used it, his vocabulary was limited.

"Shall we?" Jack said. "Our car is this way." Jordi grinned again and followed them. Since he was slightly behind them, Jack took the opportunity to check in with her. "Are you okay with this? I mean…when I go away?"

Lately, Jack had been travelling more and more for his work as a software developer. Since COVID had essentially ended, it was full bore for his company to develop new business, and meeting people face to face was a big part of that. He was going away the following week for a couple of nights, and then there was even more on the horizon

Which meant that Gabrielle would be at home alone with Jordi.

"It will be fine, I'm sure. He'll probably live in his room." She said, squeezing her husband's hand. It wasn't like she couldn't handle herself alone with a young male exchange student.

Who knew? Maybe they would have fun talking about their respective countries and she could get used to speaking Spanish at home again. "It's only six weeks."

"Okay, thank you." Jack replied. He let go of her hand and then dropped back to talk to Jordi.

's only six weeks. Six weeks of more time spent on her own, sometimes even on weekend days. She was lonely, there was no denying it. The connection they had fell into routine a long time ago and everything else had dwindled along with it.

Even driving home the conversation floated around Jordi and getting him settled into the spare bedroom. Their house wasn't massive, but it was adequate and close enough to the school for him to take a bus. It was all part of the experience of him living in another country. The fact he was a male was something they would simply have to live with.

Plus, his energy was infectious. Over dinner that night, she found herself speaking in her native tongue again often and enjoying the young man's stories about his life back home.

He was excited to be there, and excitement was something that she and Jack hadn't had in their house for quite some time. Maybe somehow their new student would give them a new sense of each other. After all, it was six weeks.

Maybe Jordi was exactly what they needed.

CHAPTER TWO

"Dammit." Gabrielle cursed. Her gym had a bad habit of substituting yoga teachers tha she didn't like. There were usually a couple of options for her to enjoy and relax herse plus get a good stretch in, and she kind of needed to release some tension. But the instructor that was standing in the room was an arrogant guy that she couldn't stand who pushed his students way too hard.

It wouldn't be enjoyable at all for her, and definitely wouldn't take care of her tense state. No point in complaining about it, but she would have to try another class anothe time.

Jack was away for another couple of days and being alone in the house with Jordi hac been fine, but slightly awkward sometimes. Her young student seemed to like to walk around the house shirtless, which was perfectly normal in some cultures, but didn't do anything to help her sexual frustration.

He wasn't massive by any means, but obviously took good care of himself and had tol them he practiced martial arts back home, so his body was lean, and his arms and stomach were well defined. It was impossible not to look sometimes. And fantasize a bit.

After all, that was harmless, right? There was no way she was ever going to act on it.

She didn't even have any errands to run, so it was probably a good idea to get home and put the laundry in to get it started. Another generic weekend day. Jordi had still been asleep when she got up and got dressed for the gym, so maybe they could figure out something fun to do together. When she pulled up to the house, she saw a car parked out front she didn't recognize.

Walking through the front door, she wondered if Jordi had a friend over from school. It was fine, of course. If they were in the living room, it would be good to meet someone else that he was in school with. Judging from the car outside, it probably wasn't a mal friend that had a pink license plate holder and a butterfly hanging from the rear-view mirror. Could it be a female friend?

That was a whole different ball game. Of course, they didn't expect Jordi to be celibate while he was in school, but asking permission to have someone of the opposite sex over was probably a good idea. Then again, he likely hadn't expected her to be home for at least another hour.

Something made her resist the urge to call out, and instead she decided to see what Jordi might be up to. If he was entertaining and hadn't asked permission, there was definitely going to be a discussion about it. Nobody was on the main floor, which mea that they were outside or upstairs. Looking out the kitchen window, the yard was empty. Which left one place. Upstairs. Whoever he had over, they were in his bedroom.

Walking slowly up the stairs, there was definitely no way the two people inside the bedroom were worried about her coming home. Because it was very clear that there was some action going on behind Jordi's closed door.

"Ai...ai...si..." she could hear quiet moans and sighs coming through the door. "...me esta tirando. Ah!"

It's stretching me? Gabrielle was having a hard enough time listening to what was going on, but once she heard those words, she realized her breath was coming short and she was sweating a bit.

The bed continued to creak, and Jordi's partner was moaning and gasping the entire time. A loud crack and a gasp echoed in the hallway. He'd spanked her and obviously, she was enjoying it.

"Si...rapido...si..." the creaking sped up and while she listened to the slap of skin against skin, Gabrielle realized she was getting damp between her legs. She was listening to two people fucking like young rabbits, and it was getting her hot. The obvious stamina and the fact that Jordi seemed to be pretty well endowed had visions flashing through her mind.

Sliding a hand under her waistband, she felt the heat in her panties and touching her pussy made her shiver slightly, goosebumps breaking out on her arm. Listening to what was going on was a thrill she didn't expect.

Her panties were easily brushed aside and when she touched her pussy lips, they were already slick. She was insanely turned on and needed some type of relief listening to what was going on behind that closed door.

"Ai...ai...dios mio...ai....si...." the young girl gasped. Her high-pitched cries were accentuated with slaps of skin and moans from both of them. She could hear Jordi moaning words as well, but couldn't make them out. Fantasizing was easy when she thought about how a passionate lover would be behaving. Seeing a young, firm body hovering over her with muscles tense and bulging as he intensely looked into her eyes and continued to ravage her.

Now Gabrielle was masturbating, unabashedly letting her hand rub her pussy while listening to the pair going at it. A lot of time had passed since she had gotten laid properly, and with Jack working so much, even the sex they had was more like a quickie than actually making love. Or getting properly fucked. She joked with her girlfriends that she needed a Costco sized box of batteries for her vibrator because she used it so often.

There was a rustle and then more sounds of moaning, and a sharp sound echoed out from behind the door. It was easy to figure out that Jordi had spanked her, and the girl was loving it. He did it again, and again, and Gabrielle wondered how good it would feel to be slapped on her ass while she was getting fucked from behind. Again, something that Jack had never done, even though they had talked about trying some kinkier stuff. Once he'd tied her hands to the bed frame, but that was about it.

Two fingers were easily sliding inside her slit, and she felt her tunnel squeezing them, pulsating inside her and giving her a rapid surge of need that went from her pussy all the way to her toes. There was no stopping what she was about to do for herself. The orgasm washed over her in a powerful wave, and she had to bite her own lip to the point of pain, unable to let the couple behind the door know she'd just cum hard all over her fingers, listening to them fuck.

It wasn't long before she heard the girl sigh again and more rustling. *"por todas mis tetas…si…si…ai…"*

Jordi let out a loud gasp and Gabrielle could hear wet sounds. Her fantasy mind told her he was jerking off a massive load of cum all over his sexy young friends' breasts, and with her fingers still idly rubbing her wet slit, she wondered how that would feel.

To have a man standing over her, furiously stroking his dick that was wet from her pussy and seeing him groan and cum in thick streams all over her naked, sweaty skin.

"Dios mio!" the girl gasped. *"es muy mucho…si…bueno."* Jordi groaned again. Finally, the sounds of movement slowed down and Gabrielle heard the creak of a bed.

Shit! She had to get out of the hallway before the couple found out she'd been listening in!

Quietly sprinting across the hall, she fled into the bedroom and got behind the door, looking through the crack to make sure that she wasn't discovered. If Jordi knew she was actually home while he'd been entertaining his girl, she had no idea how he might react.

Jordi walked out of the bedroom and Gabrielle couldn't help but look. Hanging between his legs was a dick that she almost had to look twice at to believe. Even soft, it was longer than Jack was hard, and it was thick as well, coated with a light tuft of dark hair at the base. She could see veins coursing through the dark skin and the head was almost glowing. Her breath caught, and she had to stifle a gasp.

The shaft was glistening with moisture, and it swayed between his legs while he rushed to the bathroom. Gabrielle couldn't help but watch his small but muscular ass flex while he moved. She heard the tap turn on, and then he walked back into the hallway, the gigantic dick still dangling. He was holding a washcloth and quickly scurried back into the bedroom, shutting the door.

Her entire body was tense. She'd voyeuristically observed a very intimate moment and conveniently found out that her exchange student was hung like a bull. The sound and

e fantasy of a young sexy stud pumping away was one thing, but thinking about the
ze and thickness of what he was carrying was something entirely different.

nd now she was home, and there was no way to hide it. He'd know for sure that she
eard him and his friend going at it, because it wasn't like they were being quiet about it.
ven if she'd been downstairs, it would have been audible. Gasps were very hard to
de, especially the gasps of a woman being thoroughly satisfied.

made her yearn for the days when she gave off those types of gasps when Jack was
cking her.

er body was quivering. Listening to her young student enjoy his female friend had
ven her already inflated libido a new boost, and all Gabrielle wanted to do was close
er eyes, think about his massive cock and grab her vibrator to make herself cum. At
ast twice.

ut she also wanted to enjoy it, and being interrupted wasn't going to make it what she
as craving. Unless it was being interrupted by Jordi walking into her bedroom naked,
th that massive dick getting hard between his legs.

sus, what was going on? Not only was she standing in her bedroom with dripping wet
anties under her gym clothes, but she was also actually fantasizing about a young man
at was living under their roof for at least a month longer. *Okay, Gabrielle. Time to get
ur shit together.*

e crept out of the bedroom quietly and walked back downstairs, picking up her gym
g and dropping it loudly in the front hallway. As soon as she did, there were
rambling noises from above her. Walking into the kitchen, she tried to pretend that
e'd just gotten home and busied herself making a cup of coffee as she heard
otsteps descend the stairs. Two sets of footsteps.

alking to the kitchen doorway, she saw Jordi and a beautiful girl at the bottom of the
airs. She was short, petite, and definitely stunning. Gabrielle felt a pang of jealousy.

e girl was how she looked almost twenty years ago. Deep blue eyes and long sexy
ack hair, wearing shorts that looked painted on and a crop top that left no illusions that
e was stacked. Jordi obviously had some game.

e looked at Jordi and his guilty eyes looked at her and then down at the floor. Busted.

rs. Richards! I…I didn't know you were…" he stammered. It was the first time she'd
er seen Jordi not oozing confidence. "*Este es mi amiga.*" When he declared the girl
as a friend, her eyes narrowed, and his lover shot Jordi a look that could have killed
meone.

e was standing there shirtless as usual, and now that Gabrielle knew what was
tween his legs, she couldn't help but glance down and had to stifle a smile. Quickly,
hustled the girl out the front door and when Gabrielle walked to the window, she saw

that the young girl was giving him an earful in Spanish, and the words "asshole" were definitely involved.

The front door opened after a few minutes, and then Jordi sheepishly appeared in the kitchen doorway. "Mrs. Richards. I am so sorry. I thought…"

"You thought I'd be at the gym for a while?" He nodded and looked at the floor. Truly, he looked like he was sorry for having someone over without permission.

"When did you get back?" he asked, obviously trying to make it sound innocent. Should she tell him? *Yes, Jordi. Not only did I listen to you fuck that girl senseless, but I saw the massive dick you're carrying around.*

"Just a few minutes ago. I ran some errands." She lied. He looked relieved.

"Anyway, *lo lamento*. I will ask before having people over from now on?"

"Thank you." Gabrielle replied. "It's not a problem. Is that your girlfriend?" There was no way she could be, although from her reaction at being called a friend, the poor girl definitely wanted to be.

And if his cock and skills in bed were any sign, Gabrielle knew why. He definitely worked fast, he'd only been in class for a week.

"I…uh…" he stammered.

"It's okay Jordi. I understand." Gabrielle winked at him, and he gave her a relieved smile. "I was young once too. Just make sure you let us know when you're entertaining friends."

"*Absolutamente*." He replied.

But he lingered, standing in the doorway with his eyes drifting up and down her body, and Gabrielle realized he was checking her out. She'd tried really hard to keep her body even though she was pushing forty and her yoga outfit was skimpy because it got really hot in the studio. A thought flashed through her mind.

Jordi walking up to her, pushing her against the counter and kissing her hard, feeling his big dick grinding into her and his hands all over her breasts. Passion. Lust. Need. A young stud who could probably fuck her three times and still keep going. And her husband wasn't going to be home for at least another day.

Jesus, Gabby. Stop it.

They were alone. She was horny. Nobody would ever know except the two of them. And he was massively hung, more so than any man she'd ever been with. What was holding her back? Well, her marriage for one.

If she was having fantasies about other guys, maybe it was a sign that something had to give. One way or the other. Just thinking about doing something with the young lover nder their roof was making her feel guilty, actually going through with it would be omething else entirely.

here had to be some solution. It was just a matter of figuring out what to do about her motions before they bubbled over and she did something she might regret.

istead, she quickly snapped both of them out of what she was thinking. "Is everything kay, Jordi?"

le blinked and then a different kind of smile broke over his face. A seductive one. "*Si.*" iabrielle had seen that look before. And it was something that told her his thoughts eren't far away from her own.

CHAPTER THREE

Sasha had agreed to meet her for lunch, and her best friend was somebody that she knew she could confide in without judgement. After all, Sasha had been divorced twice and was about as open about her single status as a forty-year-old woman could be.

She'd come out on the good financial end of both divorces, which meant that she could work as much as she wanted to and was always available for a lunch meeting that she claimed she could write off as a self-employed marketing guru.

They worked together a few times on PR gigs, but what Gabrielle really found her useful for was her networking skills and her blunt take on situations. She could read people like a book. And had the added benefit of being confidently stunning, evidenced every time she walked into a restaurant swaying in her Louboutin heels.

She sat down at the table and their male server took about ten seconds to run to the table. Sasha didn't even look at him. "Chardonnay. Nine ounces. Fast." He nodded and bolted away.

Gabrielle raised her eyebrows. "Rough morning, Sash? You normally don't hit the wine until after hours."

She sighed. "That fucking CMO, chief marketing asshole who thinks he knows everything. I feel like telling him if he knew what he was doing, they wouldn't be paying me several hundred dollars a day to fix his fuckups, but it is what it is. I can afford one glass. Maybe two. Jack away again?"

"Of course." She couldn't help it. Lately, it felt like he was away every week. Because he was. "He's back in a couple of days."

"Ooh, so you're alone with the Latino stud?" Sasha laughed. "I wonder if he'll try to sweep you off your feet."

"Well, he already swept some other girl off her feet yesterday." Gabrielle took a large sip of her wine.

"Damn. He's only been here for what, a week? Guy works fast. But you know those South American men." Sasha winked. "What, did he introduce her to you?"

"Yeah, after they fucked." Gabrielle took a sip of her drink as Sasha almost spit hers out.

"Oh my God, Gab! In your house? How did you find out?"

Gabrielle sighed. "I walked in on it. Well, not really. Got home from the gym and I could hear what was going on in his bedroom."

Her brow wrinkled but she still looked amused. "Wow, the kid has balls for sure. Getting laid in someone else's place. Well, he's pretty hot so I can't be surprised. Damn. So, what did you do?"

"What do you think I did? I didn't want to interrupt." Gabrielle flushed red.

Sasha laughed. "Oh my God! So, you had to listen?" She leaned in. "Was it hot? Like, hearing another couple banging? I always loved listening in. Plus, he's fucking hot. Latin lover stereotype and all. Ah, when I used to travel down there…" her wistful tone lingered.

Gabrielle couldn't help blushing, remembering how the young girl sounded behind the door. "He definitely knows what he's doing. She was making sounds I definitely haven't heard in a long time."

"I fucking knew it." Sasha crowed. "Did he eventually find out you were home?"

"Not right away. But he walked out after it was done. Fully naked. I had to hide in the bedroom, but I got a peek."

"Holy shit!" Sasha said. "So, you got to see the goods? Wow."

"And he's…well…" Gabrielle stammered.

"Spit it out, babe. He's what?"

Gabrielle flushed. "He's hung like a horse. Like a fucking Clydesdale, actually."

Sasha almost spit out the sip of her drink again, and then once she swallowed, gave a loud crow of laughter. "Holy shit, Gab! You saw him?"

Gabrielle's face was bright red. "When he came out of the bedroom. Even soft, it was bigger than Jack. Can't even imagine how big it is hard."

"And he obviously knows how to use it." Sasha mused. "Especially with some tight little Latina chick. Jesus. Mind if I take a run at him? I haven't had a young guy in a long time. You know I can barely last a couple of weeks."

"Sash!" Gabrielle laughed. "No seducing my student."

"Oh, come on. I could dress up like a teacher? Nice tight blouse and pencil skirt? How do you think I land most of my clients?" She batted her eyelashes.

"Seriously, Sash. I can't stop thinking about it." Gabrielle didn't have to even clarify what she was thinking about. Not only the way Jordi had sounded in bed, but the way he was hung.

"So maybe you should talk to Jack about it?" Sasha suggested what Gabrielle had been thinking, but it was good to hear someone else suggest something other than just diving into cheating. "Trust me babe, being open about it is always best. And considering what you've told me about your sex life, he certainly can't be surprised that you're maybe interested in a hot young guy. You guys have been having issues in that department for a while."

"I just don't want him to think he's not enough. He's a great husband. And…"

"You just need to approach it in the right way. Who knows? Maybe he'd be into it?"

Gabrielle was shocked that Sasha was so blasé about her husband and another man coming into the picture. "Into it?"

Sasha sipped her drink again. "Lots of guys are. It's called hotwifing. And the husband gets off on watching their wife fuck. They just don't want to admit it. I had a guy who loved to hear me fuck other men. He'd tell me to call him when I was hooking up with other guys and put it on speaker. Probably jerked off to it. Actually, *definitely* jerked off to it."

Gabrielle frowned. "That's kind of different from your husband. No offense."

"You think Jack's never thought about it? I mean, he travels all the time. He's not bad looking. No way he hasn't had offers. But…"

"But what?" Gabrielle felt defensive about her husband.

"Well, he's kind of a wimp when it comes to women, isn't he? I mean, it took him forever to get enough balls to ask you out way back when, right?"

That was certainly true. His boyish charm and innocence was part of what had attracted Gabrielle to him. He was totally different from the brash, aggressive men she grew up with. But that didn't mean she didn't still think about a dominant man once in a while.

Sasha continued. "I'm not trying to put him down, he's a great guy. Flirting is one thing, going through with it is something totally different. And no way Jack would ever…indulge."

That was certainly true. The major difference was that he always came home and told Gabrielle about women flirting with him, and they laughed together. But it had always sparked a bit of emotion inside her that maybe her husband was someone she had to work to keep happy. Maybe those same emotions went in the other direction as well. "He's been approached before. We've talked about it."

"And I remember at that networking party where that super hot VP was trying really hard to get under your dress. Tell me that you haven't been tempted before."

"I'm not dead, Sash. But I always come home and tell him about guys flirting with me. It's worth a laugh sometimes. I'd never cheat."

Sasha grinned. "And let me guess. If you have sex afterwards, it's extra hot?"

…e hit the nail on the head. Gabrielle remembered that night and after she'd told Jack …out the guy trying hard to pick her up, he'd suddenly wanted to tear her clothes off. …aybe it went both ways. "Well...maybe."

…asha looked at her seriously. "Long-term relationships sometimes need a bit of spice. I …ean, don't you want to introduce something that will get you laid more often? Maybe …u and Jack have a don't ask don't tell thing while he's away. Lots of couples do that …d of thing."

…eally? Lots?" Sasha grinned.

…kay, maybe not lots. But it's better than sitting at home alone with your vibrator. …pecially if you have some young big dicked stud right across the hallway. Fuck, …aybe I should take on a student." She laughed. "Or maybe I should take him out on a …d trip?" her eyebrows wiggled suggestively.

…abrielle sighed. "You really think I should talk to Jack about it?"

…bsolutely. What do you have to lose, really? If he says no, then you keep doing what …u're doing. If he says yes…" she let that part trail off and Gabrielle felt a flash of …citement. Just thinking about another man kissing her, touching her, making her feel …e a woman again, felt so naughty. "I mean, there's no way any guy would turn you …wn. You're fucking gorgeous. Guys eye fuck you all the time. There's two in this …staurant that would happily pick you up."

…was easy to ignore that side of things. Gabrielle had just gotten desensitized to it …nce she'd been married, although occasionally at yoga or somewhere else a man …uld strike up a conversation and glance down at her ring finger. And it wasn't like she …as immune to seeing other men as attractive. Her reaction to seeing Jordi shirtless …as enough evidence of that.

…ancing to her left, she saw a man suddenly turn away with a sheepish look on his …ce. Sasha was right. She was a good-looking woman and had needs. Maybe a …scussion with Jack was a good idea.

…ou just need to start the conversation, babe." Sasha said. "After all, he can't expect …u to have a crappy sex life forever."

…ur sex life isn't crappy. It's just…"

…oring. Right? Predictable? The same dick all the time? I figured out a while back …ere's probably not going to be a man who I want that from forever. At least not now."

…t how was she supposed to even bring up that she was having thoughts? Would Jack …t upset right away? Wouldn't any man if their wife told them they were having …ntasies involving other men?

It was as if Sasha read her thoughts. "You're not leaving him out. You're not having an affair. Like I said, he would be involved as much or as little as he wanted. You never know."

That was the main issue. She didn't know. First, how she would feel going ahead with letting Jordi seduce her. Or seducing him. Second, how Jack would fit into the picture was all heading in an unfamiliar direction, and Gabrielle did not know where to even begin.

The one thing she knew for sure was that she had to do something.

CHAPTER FOUR

Almost a week passed, and Jack came and went again. There was a temptation to tell him what she had heard and seen, but something inside Gabrielle made her decide to keep their students' extra activities to herself.

Things seemed to have calmed down on all fronts and she had better things to focus on. And Jordi seemed to have thrown himself back into school, or at least hadn't had anyone over at the house since he'd been caught.

That was until Gabrielle came home and again saw a strange vehicle outside their house. And it wasn't the same one as before. Quietly opening the door, she didn't know she was going to be treated to another vocal display from Jordi and another conquest. She was pleasantly surprised to see two people sitting in the living room chattering in Spanish with books out. Jordi turned and smiled.

"*Hola,* Mrs. Richards. This is Lucy. We have…a study date?" The young girl had notes in front of her at least, so there was some truth to what he was saying. But from her outfit and the way she was looking at him, there was a lot more on her mind than just reading. "I hope that is okay?"

The young girl was wearing a tight dress, almost as if she was ready to go clubbing. Definitely not something you would wear to school. Her breasts were small and perky and her makeup and hair were fully done. She almost wore a sign that screamed *Seduce Me.*

"It's fine, Jordi." Gabrielle replied. A thought percolated in her mind. "In fact, I suddenly realized I need to go out and run some errands. I'll be probably about an hour." Without letting the young girl see, she tried to use her eyes to convey that it was okay for him to do what he'd likely planned on. His eyes opened a bit wider, and she could see that he understood what she was saying. A smile broke out on his face.

"Okay, we may go and study upstairs." Gabrielle nodded and saw a look exchanged between the two of them. The girl leaned into Jordi, letting her chest become highly visible and brushing her thigh against his leg as Gabrielle gathered her purse. How long would it take him to seduce her? Probably not very long.

Of course, Gabrielle had no intention of leaving. She was only going to pretend that she was so that Jordi could do his thing with his new friend. And then she could be a voyeur, just like she had unexpectedly been the last time. Making sure to make lots of noise before she left, she quickly unlocked the back door. When she got into the car and pulled out of the driveway, she saw Jordi peeking out of the living room window, and that was evidence enough that the young pair was waiting for her to leave.

She parked down the street out of sight of the house, and then walked back, making sure that she approached the house from the side and went around to the backyard making no noise. The back door opened easily because Jack always kept things in good shape.

As soon as she walked into the kitchen and turned her ears upstairs, she could hear what was going on. A low throaty moan confirmed that Jordi had gotten straight to the point with his study partner even though it had only been minutes since she left. Gabrielle felt a thrill pass through her when she realized that Jordi's bedroom door was open. Creeping towards the stairs, she heard a gasp and then another low growl coming from Jordi. "Si…si…*chupa esa polla grande…*"

Just reaching the landing, Gabrielle positioned herself so that the door was within her view, and what she saw sent a surge straight to her thighs. Jordi was on the bed on his back, his massive thick cock straight up in the air and the young girl was running her tongue up and down the sides of his shaft, then taking just a couple of inches into her mouth.

Her hair was wild, and Jordi was holding her head, sometimes pushing his cock up between her lips. Every time he did, the girl was moaning and both of them were making intensely sexual sounds. Just the fact she was trying so hard to take his massive dick into her mouth was obviously turning her on. And Jordi was enjoying every second.

Gabrielle's mouth went dry, and she felt her panties becoming damp. What would it feel like to have that massive cock head spreading her lips and feel inch after inch invading her mouth, stretching it to the point of feeling uncomfortable? Licking up and down the massive shaft that probably smelled so manly and musky? Having him pulling on her hair, urging her to take even more?

She watched his hands twine into her hair, and then with forceful movements the girl started to gasp and choke slightly as Jordi fucked her mouth and throat with ease. Pulling herself off with a gasp, his hands pulled her up and he kissed her hard, moaning into her mouth, then shoved her back down and pushed his cock back into her waiting mouth. Taking control, just like Gabrielle suspected he would.

The young girl continued to suck him, moaning with her eyes closed until Jordi pulled her easily off his dick. He shoved her down onto the bed and the girl eagerly lifted her hips, allowing him to reach underneath and pull her panties off. He tossed them onto the floor without a second thought.

Climbing on top of her, the girl opened her legs and then lifted them up, wrapping them around Jordi as he skimmed his pants down lower and Gabrielle could see his firm ass flexing with perfectly shaven balls. She was obviously eager to get to the main event.

Like she had before, Gabrielle had to touch herself. Her pussy was humming with need watching the two young lovers together, like a live action sex show that was just for her

And the star of the show was Jordi's massive cock, hard as steel and ready to penetrate his lover.

Lining up his cock, the girl underneath him looked up at him, biting her lip. *"Ve lenta…es tan grande…"*

Go slow. It's so big. Jordi's hips moved and suddenly the young girl gave out a loud wail as he pushed forward inside her. Gabrielle almost came on the spot with one finger inside her, her mind racing what it would feel like to take a cock that big inside her for the first time. Jordi pulled out slightly and gently pushed in again, the girl now clutching at his back and gasping high pitched little squeals as he worked his cock deep inside her inch by massive inch.

Moving her hand faster in her pants, Gabrielle couldn't help it. All she could think about was the penetration she was witnessing and how much pleasure the young girl was getting from Jordi's massive cock. Her clit was throbbing with need and skimming her palm over it was enough to make her body surge towards her own completion.

Once Jordi was inside completely, he began to fuck the young girl steadily, and she was giving little guttural gasps every time he moved. Like a symphony, the sounds of pleasure filled the air inside the house. Gabrielle couldn't stop herself. She needed to feel something. Two fingers slid into her wet slit easily and quickly, and she held on to the railing of the stairs while she blatantly finger fucked herself.

Thankfully the sounds of the two young people fucking covered up the sounds of her wet pussy with fingers moving inside it. It was insane how wet she was, her pants almost soaking through with desire as the sexual display continued only meters away.

Jordi pulled out, tugged his pants off and then grabbed the girl by the waist, jerking her towards the edge of the bed. His hand flipped her onto her stomach, and then Gabrielle watched his muscles flex as he pulled her into position to enter her from behind.

Before he did, she saw his cock fully hard. It was breathtaking. Long and firm, coated with his partner's cum. It seemed almost impossibly big, but he definitely wielded it like an expert, lining it up against her and then thrusting into her from behind. Just imagining a man's gigantic cock entering her that hard and deep in one thrust made Gabrielle's pussy surge, and she realized she was about to cum all over her hand.

As the couple in the bedroom kept fucking, she moved a hand to her mouth and bit down on it gently, stifling the cry she felt she needed to release as her pussy bore down on her fingers and her orgasmic contractions shook her entire body. Dripping wetness engulfed her fingers. Her legs got weak suddenly, and it was a good thing she was holding onto the railing, otherwise she might have fallen down the stairs.

As her vision cleared, she watched enraptured as Jordi gave out a loud bellow of sexual release and then pulled his massive dick out of his partner's gaping pussy, erupting with a massive cumshot across her ass and back. The girl laid forward, her hands clutching the sheets in her hands and mewling little gasps in front of him.

Jordi took the head of his dick and spread around the cum he'd just let go. *"tan jodidamente sexy"* So fucking sexy. He wasn't wrong about that. His cock slapped against her ass a couple of times and both of them sighed in a satisfied way that told Gabrielle both were thoroughly happy.

Like he had before, Jordi stepped away, and his massive cock, still lengthy and glistening, bobbed between his legs as he walked towards his bedroom door. Gabrielle went rigid. She was about to be discovered if she didn't move fast.

Almost scrambling down the stairs, she ran into the kitchen and then paused. Jordi's footsteps stopped at the top of the stairs, and she waited, trying to quiet her breathing. He took one step down and then the girl called out from the bedroom.

Gabrielle gave a relieved breath out when he stepped back up and headed to the bathroom. She opened the back door again without an issue and headed back to her car, her legs shaking as she walked.

What she'd witnessed wasn't only an invasion of Jordi's privacy, but it was a display of sexual prowess she couldn't deny she wanted to experience. With Jack away all the time, could she bring herself to allow their young student into her bed? To fuck her into oblivion like she had just witnessed him do to another woman?

She had to talk to Jack. If he gave her the all clear, then it was up to her to make the decision that could change her sexual life and their marriage, maybe for the better.

CHAPTER FIVE

e next time Jack was home, Gabrielle had resigned herself to finally bringing up the
phant in the room. Although it was one he likely didn't expect. The night he got back
bed, she was still thinking about listening to Jordi and watching his second conquest
d it steeled her resolve to figure out something.

/e need to talk about something." Gabrielle said as she climbed into bed. Jack looked
her with raised eyebrows.

hat doesn't sound good." But at least he put his tablet away and was taking her
riously. "What's going on? Is everything okay?"

/e need to talk…about our sex life."

ck grimaced, and she had hoped that wouldn't be his reaction. He worked long hours,
at she knew, and he was a fantastic partner. But the physical side of things between
em had drifted into an abyss, and they both knew it. "Listen. I know you're working
ur butt off, and things have been insanely stressful. I'm not saying that I want to put
y added pressure on you. I just need…"

ore sex?" he laughed. "Trust me babe, I do too."

e took his hand. "Babe, it's not like I don't want you. It just seems like everything is
tting in the way lately. But I want to try to fix it."

s funny. Most guys would be ecstatic to hear that. And I know I haven't exactly been
eping up my part in our sex life. I've just been…"

eally busy and preoccupied. I know, babe, and that's actually not what this is all
out." She said, "Of course, I want to have more sexy time with you, but since maybe
at's not possible for the time being, I was wondering…"

e took a deep breath. It was time to say what she had rehearsed in her mind over
d over, but it was much more difficult to say out loud. *Hey, I want to fuck someone
se.*

o maybe you would be okay with…me having some fun. Without you. I mean, you're
ay a lot and…"

ck looked startled and it looked like she'd punched him in the gut as he processed
at she had just said out loud. Finally, he spoke. "I know things haven't been the best
ely. But I guess I never thought it was that bad?"

abrielle took his hand and squeezed it. "But that's why we need to have the
nversation. I would rather talk about it and deal with it together than…well…"

heat on me?"

She flushed. "I'd never do that."

He squeezed her hand back. "Okay, so let's deal with it. I know I travel a lot. Does that mean we need to get on a more frequent sex schedule when I'm home? Like, what does having fun mean? Video sex? You want to buy a new toy?"

Gabrielle knew he was trying to avoid the subject she'd just brought up. The idea that she wanted to introduce some kind of outside element into their marriage. A new dildo wasn't going to do it.

It was time to broach the subject she knew might throw a wrench into the works. The item that could make or break their relationship, and if he refused outright Gabrielle would just have to honor it and figure something else out. She'd rehearsed the words hundred times in her mind but saying them was more difficult than she had expected.

"I'm wondering how you would feel about me…exploring outside of just us?"

His brow furrowed, and then he sighed. "You mean like an open marriage."

"Well, kind of…I think? I'm not exactly good at this either." Gabrielle squeezed his hand again. "I guess part of me hoped that if I did something with someone else, I could…share it with you."

"Is there somebody else you're thinking about already?" the words sounded slightly accusatory, and that was understandable.

"No." Gabrielle lied. "Not at all. I just…I've been thinking about it."

"I don't know how to feel about that." Jack said simply. "So you mean if you…meet up with someone, or someone makes a move on you and you do something with them, you tell me about it?"

She took another deep breath. "Or, you could watch? I've read up on it and sometimes the husbands enjoy watching their wives get…pleasured." She wanted to say fucked, but it seemed crude. "I know you enjoy watching me sometimes when I masturbate, so this would be another step in that direction."

Jack laughed. "Yeah, except another guy is fucking my wife."

Gabrielle decided to see if she could push the envelope slightly in her favor. She slid a hand under the sheets and when she moved it onto his crotch, Jack went tense. Squeezing him, she started to slide her hand up and down. "Just listen for a second. I know you love watching me suck your cock, right?" His penis stiffened quickly under the light pressure of her caress.

"Uh…yeah, definitely." Now he was hard enough for her to wrap her hand around his shaft, and she slid her hand over and around the head. He had always enjoyed that. She slid closer to him and tucked her head against his chest while she continued to touch him.

So maybe imagine watching me sucking…using my tongue…hearing me moan while I ride my lips all the way down the shaft…" His cock had gotten fully hard and now she could feel him trembling. Moving her hand to his waistband, she pushed underneath and encircled his rigid shaft, pumping lightly as he hissed in his throat. "Wow, you're getting so hard."

"It's fucking hard…not to be with you jerking me off." Jack sighed. "But…tell me more." His shaft flexed in her hand.

Perfect.

She squeezed harder and used her hand around the spongy head, slowly stroking him. "Imagine watching me on my knees…licking and sucking on a nice hard cock like you have right now…" He groaned and pushed his hips up when she said the word watched. "Just close your eyes and imagine it."

Jack closed his eyes and Gabrielle continued to tease his dick, sliding her hand all the way up and down his shaft and enjoying his reaction to what she was doing. "Can you picture it? Watching your wife suck a cock like you like watching?"

"God…babe…yes, I can picture it."

It was time to push the envelope further. "So, think about me naked. Ready to enjoy getting fucked. Watching me bend over and spread my legs. I'd be so wet. Just waiting for that nice big dick to slide inside me."

As she talked, she tugged on his pants, and Jack's dick sprung free, sticking up harder than she had seen it in a long time. Gabrielle threw the sheets aside. "I want it. I want this inside me, baby."

"Come and get it." Jack groaned. She slid across his body, knowing that her nightgown would ride up and her panties rubbed against his shaft. Then she realized how wet she was. Just like the throbbing hardness of his erection, her pussy was dripping wet, wetter than she could remember being in a while. As wet as she had been when listening to Jordi having sex in the other room.

Her panties easily moved aside, and she slid up his body, letting the head sink inside her. They both gasped and with a simple push, Jack's cock filled her up. It was familiar and lovely, and she felt the shivers that always coursed through her body whenever they were together. But in the back of her mind, she was thinking about the massive dick she had seen the other day. Wondering how it would feel.

How much deeper would it go? Enough to push against her deepest depths? Would it feel fuller? Stretch her? Be painful? As she moved up and down and Jack grabbed her breasts, she sat up and took off her nightgown.

"Fuck, you're so gorgeous." He sighed.

Leaning down, Gabrielle kissed him hard and then leaned over to whisper in his ear. "Now just imagine watching me riding someone…seeing my breasts…hearing me moan…seeing a cock covered with my pussy."

Jack turned his head away, but hissed and pushed up into her. "Fuck…"

"God, he feels so good fucking me with his big dick." Maybe that was slightly too far. At least until she heard his response.

"Yeah? You like getting fucked with another man's cock?" Jack pushed up into her again, hard and deep. His words came out in a guttural growl and Gabrielle knew he was enjoying thinking about it.

"He feels so good, baby. That big cock is making me feel so good. I think I'm going to cum." Gabrielle moved a hand between their joined bodies and found her clit, throbbing and sensitive. Rubbing it softly, there was a surge of excitement and tension inside her. "Fuck, yes…he's going to make me cum so hard. I'm so fucking hot."

"Cum for me, baby…" Jack moaned. Rubbing slightly faster, Gabrielle felt her body go tense and then begin the glorious shiver that her orgasm always brought. It had been a long time since they had one together, and this one was fantastic. She gasped into his ear and let her lips find his neck, gently unable to stop herself from biting down. At the same time, Jack let out a loud groan and she felt his cock flex, emptying inside her as she continued to drift up and down his shaft.

"Holy shit…" he said. His breath and hers were coming in short pants. Turning her head Gabrielle looked into a pair of hazy eyes and then Jack kissed her hard. With passion she could feel right down to her toes.

Moving off him, she slid back into the position where she'd begun stroking him and gently slid his pyjama pants back up with a smile. She slid next to him. "Wow, babe…that was…"

"That was fucking amazing." Jack sighed in response. His head turned, and the haze had left his eyes. Then they turned more serious, and he sat up. "But…do you think it might work? I mean, do you think we could get into a place where I could watch you with someone else?"

"Maybe." Gabrielle had to stop herself from just jumping in. "Let's take it one step at a time." That seemed to satisfy Jack, and she slid out of the bed to head to the bathroom. Once she returned, he was already breathing heavily and asleep. Her mind was still racing, but somehow, she felt both relieved and relaxed at the same time. They had gotten through the first hurdle. And she could begin to think about exploring like she had hoped she might.

After all, if his reaction to her words was any indication of how good the sex could be afterwards, actually going through with it might be even more explosive. For both of them.

CHAPTER SIX

The slight haze from a couple of glasses of wine was steeling Gabrielle's resolve. After their conversation about opening up the marriage, and the incredible sex she and Jack had shared afterwards, she felt like she was ready to let her inhibitions out and simply see where it went.

They had established a couple of ground rules, which, when they began talking about it almost made her laugh. Apparently, Jack had done some research on the subject, which was pretty typical for him.

No penetration was allowed, at least not yet. He wasn't willing to allow that to happen, but told her it would depend on how things went. Nothing in their main bedroom with another man. Gabrielle had to be completely open about everything that happened as soon as possible after whatever occurred. Those were both no problem at all for her. She was still intensely nervous and what she was about to do, which was seduce a younger man for the first time.

Even though Jordi had shown signs he thought she was attractive, there was always the chance he would shoot her down. Which would be a massive blow to her ego. It wasn't like he wasn't getting laid just fine on his own. But Gabrielle almost took it as a challenge. There was no way in the dress she wore a guy would resist her coming on to him. Would he?

The situation was perfect. Jack was away for a couple of nights, and Jordi seemed to stick around the house for the evening. He'd told Gabrielle he had a big test the following day so needed to study, and she told him he could use the living room because she had some things she wanted to do in her bedroom before heading to a networking event later.

What she really was doing was getting her confidence up. After all, she was an older woman and definitely not flawless and she was about to seduce a young man who had proven he could basically get laid whenever he pleased. With much younger, more attractive women.

But he'd shown interest, right? And with the dress she had picked out, there was no way possible he was going to resist her. It was far more risqué than anything she would have ever worn to a professional event. The plunging neckline alone was enough, but it molded to her curves and was cut very high above the knee.

She even had to be careful sitting down, otherwise she'd flash whoever was sitting near her who had the proper angle.

Fluffing out her hair, she brushed it gently, so it flowed over her shoulders and applied some makeup to make her eyes shine and her cheeks stand out. Looking at herself,

e lifted her breasts. *Still got it.* Jack would have lost his mind seeing her in the dress
d wouldn't have been able to keep his hands off her. And here she was hoping
other young man would have the same reaction.

sat there with a book on the table, making notes, and as Gabrielle walked into the
om, she saw his eyes look her up and down. The dress she was wearing was
finitely one of her hottest numbers. Tight, leaving no curve untouched and without a
a on, she felt every bit the seductress.

ter putting it on, she knew going out into public would be interesting, and seeing men
nstantly checking her out, as Sasha had pointed out, had just fueled the fire inside
r she needed to be seduced. Or wanted to seduce someone. Thinking about it for
ur had made her desperately horny.

r heels clicked along the floor and Jordi looked up and then did a double take when
saw the dress she wore. Perfect. "*Hola,* Mrs. Richards."

ola, Jordi. Studying?"

nodded and smiled that cocky smile. "*Si.* We have a test tomorrow. I still have to
ake sure my grades stay strong."

was time. Gabrielle sat down beside him. "Maybe you should take a bit of a break."
s eyes found hers and she could see him searching for what she might mean. "Relax
a bit. With me."

quickly snapped the book closed. "I would love to, Mrs. Richards." Getting closer to
n, Gabrielle could tell he was being careful about making the first move. She was
ing hard to be completely transparent about her intentions, as if the dress wasn't
ough.

all me Gabrielle, Jordi." She leaned closer and Jordi tensed up noticeably. How was it
ssible that the younger man was suddenly shy around her, after she'd seen him bring
me a couple of stunning women to their house? "I think you can call me Gabrielle
en it's just the two of us."

e slid closer and while he didn't shy away, he certainly didn't seem to know what to
about her. Which was honestly kind of surprising. "I know what I would like to do."

h, yes? And what is that?" his eyes dropped to her breasts and Gabrielle reached out
touch his hand. "I can think of something we can do together." His hand wrapped into
rs and suddenly their fingers were intertwined. Just that slight amount of contact
ade her panties damp. He looked at her inquisitively. "But, Mr. Richards?"

on't worry, Jack is away. And I think we both know what we want. I've been wanting
get to know you better. Close." She knew that she would have to be the one making
e first move, and all she could hope was that once she opened him up to the idea, he
uld be okay with it. After all, she'd heard him take charge with his other women. She

let her hand slide across his pants and when she felt how big he was already, her body heated.

"Mrs…I mean, Gabrielle. What are you doing?" his eyes darted to her hand, then to her eyes and back again. He was being very careful to not be the one that was aggressive. She was in charge of what was happening. "Are you okay with this?" His dick flexed under her hand and Gabrielle had to stifle a moan in her throat at the fact she was finally touching him.

Having the element of control was actually making her even hotter. Suddenly she could feel the powerful sense that she was taking control of him and if she just allowed herself to be aggressive, she could get exactly what she was craving. Her panties were soaked.

"Like I said, Jordi. Don't worry about Jack. Let's just enjoy ourselves." Her hand found his zipper and when she tugged on it and it came down, his hips bucked against her hand again. His eyes found hers again, and they were wide and innocent looking but quickly changed into deep desire.

When she reached inside his fly and felt how hard he was, Gabrielle knew his hormones had taken over. He moaned when she touched him through his underwear.

His cock was long and warm. As she moved her hand, she realized it could barely fit inside her grip. Looking down at it barely covered, she was salivating. "Just relax. Let me enjoy you."

He nodded, and Gabrielle took that as permission. She undid his belt and tugged at his pants. With a gasp from her, his cock finally came into full view, and it was spectacular. Full, thick and hard. At least a couple of inches longer than Jack, and as she squeezed it in her hand, the idea that her grip wouldn't fit was confirmed. And it wasn't like she had small hands.

And so hard, it felt alive in her hand. Pumping with blood, veiny and glorious. At the very tip was a small bead of clear fluid. Using her thumb, she spread the slick droplet around his cock head and Jordi groaned. "Ay…Miss…Gab…"

It was so big. Just stroking him slowly and seeing how much hard cock was in her hand had her body feeling shaky. Giving him a blow job like she'd intended was daunting because she wasn't sure he'd even fit. She kept slowly moving her hand up and down and watched as he closed his eyes, then opened them and stared at her chest.

Her heart was hammering. Was she really going to go through with what she'd intended? It was time to throw caution to the wind and enjoy what she had started. Leaning down, she let her lips wrap around his spongy head and her mouth stretched accommodate his massive size. Her jaw actually felt sore.

Jordi let out a loud groan and as she bobbed her head and tried to let her mouth get used to his enormous size, he grabbed her hair and stroked it. Letting her tongue slide around him, she licked the underside of his shaft and felt the veins skip across her taste

ıds. He even smelled good and as they both settled into what was happening, she
arted to enjoy herself.

pparently he was as well, because he moaned and then lay back slightly, positioning
ımself so he could enjoy watching her and smiling. "I have…did not know you
ere…interested." He breathed. "What about Mister Richards?" he asked again, as if
eeding even more reinforcement that he wasn't going to get kicked out of the house.

fting her mouth off him with a pop, Gabrielle smiled at him. "Don't worry about him. We
ave an understanding." She sucked his head gently again and enjoyed when he
asped as her lips moved on his skin.

have…ah…heard about this." Jordi sighed. "You are so beautiful."

earing another man say that she was beautiful, especially while she was sucking his
ɔck, made Gabrielle shudder with desire. He was responding perfectly, letting her
ıjoy his nice, thick cock while complimenting her. Jack took it for granted and simply
t her go to town, always making sure he warned her before he was about to pop. And
at never took long.

rying to take the biggest cock she'd ever sucked even deeper, Gabrielle pushed down
ıtil she felt it graze the back of her throat and almost choke her, making her breath
atch. It sent a rush of adrenaline through her, and Jordi gasped.

'eeeessss…" he moaned. "So fucking good…you are so sexy, Gabby."

oh, a nickname. She lifted her mouth off him and then kissed the tip of his cock,
niling up at him. "Are you enjoying this?"

ři. Muy bueno." He smiled back. Gabrielle pumped his cock a few more times and
:ked another delicious drop of precum off his tip.

.et me see your tits." He said. Without any hesitation, Gabrielle slid down first one
rap and then the other, letting her breasts free. Jordi's hand grabbed his own cock as
e looked at her. "Ai…fantastica. Esplendido."

/ith the long cock offered to her, Gabrielle couldn't resist. She slid forward and her his
ɔck graze her nipples, then slid his massive length between her breasts. It was so
ng, as she moved her chest back and forth and masturbated his glorious cock she
ɔuld lick the head. He groaned again and began to move his hips, fucking the cleavage
ıe was eagerly offering him.

want to make you cum." She meant it. All Gabrielle could think about was letting
ıother man erupt into her mouth and throat. To see what he tasted like. Taking him
rmly between her lips again, she sucked and let her tongue glide around the thickness
ıat threatened to unhinge her jaw with its' massive girth.

loving faster, she was rewarded with more moaning from her new young stud, and his
ps began to move. His hands flew to the couch, and she glanced to see them

clutching at the pillows while his pants became close knit and fierce. It was obvious he was intensely enjoying it. Increasing the pressure, she kept going, craving for his seed to flood her mouth.

Grabbing him by the base, she stroked him while she sucked and knew from the pulsir in her mouth he was close. Normally with Jack, she would have simply removed her mouth and let him cum on himself, but this was different. This was a young man about to unleash his massive load into her throat.

When she felt him flex, she slid her mouth down and the first spray of cum hit her throa almost threatening to choke her. Opening her mouth a bit, she swallowed quickly befor another spurt flowed into her mouth. The taste was so different than what she was use to, and she was thrilled to sense that it was sweet and thick.

The noises coming from his mouth were guttural and low, and his hips were shaking lik a leaf while Gabrielle closed her mouth again and sucked gently, feeling one more dollop of his thick cum slide onto her tongue. Swallowing that, she lifted her head and laughed with the thrill of what she had just done. Jordi leaned back and arched, letting out a loud sigh as he looked down at her and smiled.

Even as she continued to stroke him, the taste in her mouth didn't diminish. The thrill o what she'd just done had her whole body quivering with excitement. His dick deflated slightly, but the length in her hand remained the biggest she'd ever touched even while partly soft.

"Wow. Gabby." Jordi said with another broad smile. "I was not expecting that." He sat up, and with no warning, he lifted Gabrielle by the chin and kissed her. His tongue slid into her mouth, and, with no hesitation, she welcomed it.

The kiss was passionate and deep and lusty, and while he kissed her, she felt his hand move to her chest and squeeze her breasts. The nipples were rock hard, and his thumbs skated across them, making her shiver.

Jesus, he wants more. Gabrielle was torn. It had definitely gone as far as she intended in fact, even further. Things were rapidly getting out of control, and the problem was th. she was insanely horny and could only think about the idea of their bodies sliding together and his massive dick ravaging her pussy, which was dripping wet and eager t be claimed.

He pushed her back as they kissed, and quickly his hand moved between her legs. As soon as he touched her panties, she realized how drenched they were. Soaked. And h easily brushed them aside and slid a finger down her slit, then inside her pussy, makin; her gasp into his mouth and her hips quiver.

Breaking the kiss, his finger explored her folds while his eyes met hers, full of lust. "I want to taste you."

Gabrielle couldn't help but nod, and quickly he was sliding his head between her legs and had her panties aside. The tongue that suddenly entered her pussy made an electric bolt shoot up her spine, and when she gasped out loud, it was enough for people walking by on the sidewalk to hear. She had no idea how good it felt to have a man passionately eating her out.

Apparently, the idea of the Latin lover was really damned accurate, because Jordi feasted on her pussy like it was his last meal. And his tongue felt like it was sending a conduit of pleasure straight up to her brain and back down, causing her body to quiver like ripples on a pond. He was moaning and sighing as if she was delicious.

It was everywhere, exploring each side of her sensitive opening and then plunging inside as if tasting her nectar, then swirling around her clit and teasing her to the edge before dancing away and making her feel like she wanted to beg him to make her cum.

Now she knew why she'd heard such intense noises from the women he entertained, because she heard herself making the same guttural sounds of intense delight that his other lovers did. How was it possible that such a young man was so skilled with his tongue and lips? And he was giving the best pussy eater she'd ever experienced a run for his money.

Finally giving her a chance to breathe, he looked up at her, and Gabrielle gave him a hazy smile. "I want to feel you *coom*. On my tongue." And with that, he dove back in, finding her outer lips and tracing a delicate path up each one, again circling her clit with the skill of an artist using a paintbrush. Within moments Gabrielle could feel every inch of her contracting with intensity and she gasped, unable to stop herself from grabbing his head and clutching at his hair. *Holy shit.*

Like a runaway freight train, her orgasm overwhelmed her senses, and she bucked her hips wildly up into Jordi's face, crying out with a high-pitched squeal she hadn't heard herself make before. The shudders threatened to make her legs cramped, and she twitched violently on the couch, unable to contain how good her young lover had just made her feel. As she lay there panting, he licked gently at the juices that were flowing out of her, and then lifted his head and grinned at her. "*Muy caliente.*"

"Si." Gabrielle sighed. "Muy fucking caliente. Jesus." she closed her legs and somehow slid herself into a seated position, feeling slightly lightheaded. The impact of what she had just allowed to happen hit her. Not only had she given a young student living under her roof a blowjob, she'd also let him go down on her and make her...well, explode, frankly. Like a bomb. If he could do that with his mouth, just imagine how good his massive cock was going to feel.

"I think maybe I will like it when Mister Richards is away." Jordi tucked himself back into his pants and then leaned in, but Gabrielle leaned away. Even after what had happened, she didn't want to give him the wrong impression.

"That was very fun, Jordi. But it will only happen when I allow it to." She tried to make her expression as serious as possible. "And only when Mister Richards is away." *Or maybe in the room.* He nodded with a massive smile.

"No problem, Gabby. I will restrain myself. I hope." He grinned again, but the way his eyes looked at her now told her he was also steps away from doing what they both wanted. Using his cock to make her scream with pleasure. Just his expression made her shudder with need. She had to get away from him.

"Okay then. You have studying to do." Gabrielle got up and rearranged her clothing, knowing she needed to use some mouthwash as well. Even though the taste that was inside her mouth was giving her a thrill just being there.

Jordi disappeared inside his bedroom, and Gabrielle busied herself for the rest of the evening in hers. It felt awkward to be in her own house now, and that was an odd feeling. She didn't know how to feel about what had happened, but the thrill of it persisted even a couple of hours later. Part of her wanted Jordi to just walk into her bedroom, and if he was aggressive enough about it, she might let her last barrier down.

She had to tell Jack. He had given her permission, that was true, and she knew he was expecting an update. But it was hard to press the call button and think about telling him she'd just given their young student a blowjob. And the part about him devouring her until she almost screamed was definitely something she should leave out. Right?

She pressed the call button. Jack answered almost right away. "Hey, babe. What's up?"

"It happened." The pause on the other end of the line went on for far too long.

"What happened?"

"What we talked about."

"Like, you and...someone else? Jesus, babe, we've only been talking about it for a week." He was chuckling, but Gabrielle could tell he was slightly upset.

"It wasn't really someone else. Just someone convenient." He paused again.

"You mean...you and Jordi?"

"Yes."

"Did he come on to you?"

"No, I came on to him. He's made it pretty obvious he's attracted to me and I thought maybe it would be a good way to...dip my toes in the water?" It was a stupid way to phrase what she'd done, but now that it was out in the open, she had to figure out the next steps. "Are you upset?"

"I'm not upset. Just a bit surprised, I guess. I mean, he's a good looking guy."

e's been having girls over. And I've heard them more than once. I didn't tell you, but
 seems to be insanely good with women."

nd now I guess you can confirm that." Jack laughed again.

ut I want to share it all with you, like we talked about." Gabrielle told him. "That's an
portant part of this. And…" she paused. "…there's details I want to share with you.
ll you all about it."

ang on, let me close my door. I'm still at the office, but nobody is around. Just making
re." She could hear him almost running across the office. "Okay. I'm ready. Tell me.
nat happened?" His voice was apprehensive, but Gabrielle took a deep breath and
gan talking.

e was studying on the couch in the living room. I put on that blue dress you like."

ne tight one?"

es."

nd?"

nd…I saw down next to him. We talked a bit. And then…I started to touch him."

ang on." She heard a distinct jingle. Jack had undone his pants. That was a good
n. "You touched him? Like how?"

ubbed his crotch. He was already hard. God, babe, his dick is big. Like, gigantic."

ow do you know that?"

ecause I took his pants off and he was hard as a rock. It was insane how long and
rd he was."

uuck." Jack sighed. "It's actually making me hard just thinking about it. Did you…kiss
n?"

'e kissed…after I was done. I took him out and then gave him a really slow blow job.
 barely fit in my mouth. My jaw is sore." She could hear sounds of Jack masturbating,
 obvious noise of his belt buckle and friction. And she could feel herself getting wet
ain just describing what had happened between the two of them. "Are you jerking
?"

es." He said. "How long did you suck him for?"

long time." Now she was getting into it. "He was pulling my hair and moaning. I was
fucking turned on, Jack."

et you were. Such a wicked wife, sucking another man's cock. Were you wearing
nties under the dress?"

She got creative. "Yes. I was gushing. So fucking wet while I sucked his big dick."

"Shhiiiittt..." Jack gasped. "Could you take it all?"

"No way. It's too long and thick. My mouth feels so stretched out, babe. All I could thin about was how much I wanted him to fuck me."

"Yeah? You want him to fuck you? Hard and deep with that big cock? Make him cum? Did he cum in your mouth?"

"I kept sucking him hard and licking his shaft and then jerking him off with my hand, swirling it around."

"God, I love that. You always make me pop in two minutes."

"He was trying to last, but eventually he had to cum. And I let him cum in my mouth."

"Fuck!" Jack gasped. "You're so bad, babe. Did you swallow?" She could hear the sounds of his masturbation speeding up over the phone line.

"Every drop. I can still taste it. There was so much it dripped out of my lips. He came like a fountain in your sexy wife's mouth. Cum dripping down my lips, onto my tits and covering them. I was almost naked for him."

"Ahh...ah...fuck, I'm going to cum." Jack gasped. "I'm fucking cumming thinking about you sucking off another man!"

"Cum for me, baby. Let that cock explode." Gabrielle sighed. There was a sudden bla pause of sound and then a rush of breath in her ear. "Yes...that's so good...cum for me."

A long silence came as she heard heavy breathing into the phone. The thrill was unmistakeable. She'd just confessed sucking off another man and her husband had enjoyed it.

"Fuuuck...holy shit. I just came all over myself. Jesus." His breath was coming in shor bursts. "I've never done that before."

"What?" Gabrielle giggled. "Jerked off with your wife?"

"Jerked off in my office with my wife, telling me about doing something with another man." Jack replied, and the impact of the statement hung in the air, even over a telephone line. He quickly added another sentence. "But I kind of liked it."

"Me too." Gabrielle said. "It's really hot to know you just did that." And it was the truth. wasn't like she didn't want him to be satisfied as well, and after all, she had received own satisfaction only a little earlier thanks to her young lover. "I think maybe we are o the right track."

"Definitely." Jack sighed. "So maybe we can...keep going."

ne words keep going also hung in the air. What did that even mean? Was she allowed give Jordi more oral satisfaction and get it for herself? Could they think about more?

Does that mean you're okay with me and Jordi exploring things?" It was definitely an ephant in the room. After all, he was under their roof and Gabrielle had access to him d his glorious dick anytime she wanted.

have to think about it. But I'm okay with what happened." Having his reassurance ave her a flush of relief.

guess we'll talk when you get home."

Absolutely." Jack said. "Now I have to clean up this mess." Gabrielle laughed.

When she hung up the call, her mind was still racing, but she knew one thing: that she'd oroughly enjoyed what had happened. And she definitely wanted to experience it gain. Possibly even more. As soon as she could.

CHAPTER SEVEN

Their home was in full swing for the nights' party, and Gabrielle was happy to have something to keep her mind off things. When she realized what she had gone through with the next day after enjoying being with Jordi, it was almost as if she went into a panic. She'd betrayed her husband and her marriage vows. Even though he knew abo it. And had even jerked off hearing about it.

A saving grace was that Jordi seemed to be completely ignoring the situation and had simply accepted his good fortune at being seduced by her that one time. The insane orgasm that he'd given her with his tongue hadn't left her mind. Even though he was young, Gabrielle could tell he'd earned every moan and exclamation she'd heard from his other two lovers.

And that dick. Oh my. So massively big, so delicious and so hot, watching and feeling him cum down her throat. Then afterwards, knowing that Jack was getting off as well. Was it wrong? Maybe. But wow, was it ever hot. And because they were being open about it, there wasn't anything wrong going on.

The party was a weekend thing they'd had planned for a while, and Jordi being there was just part of adding to the festivities. He was happy to meet their friends and participate in setting things up, even preparing a dip that he said his mother made at home. It was absolutely delicious. Once the party had begun, Gabrielle welcomed the distraction.

With twenty people in the house, including some of Jordi's friends from school, there was no way to take a pause. Thankfully, he hadn't invited either of the other young ladies that he'd seduced before her, so Gabrielle didn't have to deal with any potential drama if they found out what had happened between them. The young students were mostly hanging out on their own in the backyard and enjoying some music. Jack was tending the barbecue and Gabrielle was running around, trying to make sure everyone had food and drink.

She'd worn a simple summer dress because of the weather and as soon as Sasha showed up with a bottle of Prosecco in hand, she'd whistled. "Damn, girl. I guess you took what I said to heart! Every guy here is going to be checking you out all night."

That included her husband, who was being surprisingly affectionate when she drifted b the barbecue. More than once he'd wrapped his arm around her waist and kissed her i front of the entire party, and usually public displays were not his thing.

When he'd arrived home after his trip, they had mostly gone back to their old routine, not even really talking about what had happened. She could tell that he wasn't ready, and frankly, neither was she. Both of them needed to process the fact that they'd had such an intense first time, including somebody else in their sexual fun. And he was being much more affectionate, even flirtatious sometimes.

The wine was flowing and the Latin themed music had her feeling good. Taking a moment to step away, she headed upstairs to their ensuite to freshen up her makeup and adjust her dress.

Damn, I look good. It was a good sign that Jack was being extra affectionate, and maybe after everyone was gone, they could finally get into bed and enjoy some fun without the spectre of Jordi hanging over their head. Unless that was how they needed to have fun with each other. Maybe if she started telling him about what happened again he'd have the same response.

The bathroom door opened quickly, startling her, and without warning Jordi stepped inside, closing it behind him. Gabrielle looked at him through the mirror and suddenly she knew what he was there for without him having to say a word. Her body went tense but when she saw the look in his eye, she couldn't deny her body responding. Her pussy twitched. "Jordi…what are you doing in here?"

Without giving an answer, he walked up behind her. Gabrielle knew exactly what he had in mind, and the idea of them fooling around while her husband and a dozen other people were downstairs was insane. "I can't stay away, Gabby. Ever since you pleasured me, I have been craving you." The look in his eye was unmistakable. It was pure lust, and he wasn't about to be denied. She tensed up as he closed the distance between them and suddenly was inside her personal space. A lot inside. Close enough for his chest to touch hers.

His hands dropped and then slid up the sides of her dress, lifting it and exposing her ass cheeks. She could smell his breath and the scent of his cologne, and if they both leaned in, they could be kissing. There was no hesitation as he moved her dress to expose her bare legs, stroking the skin of her hips and making her nipples pebble in and instant. And her panties were hot.

She made a half-hearted attempt to slap his hands away. "Hey. Stop it. Not now. Not here."

Her words were completely ignored. There was no stopping him. Quickly spinning her around to face the mirror, he dropped to his knees, and with her dress lifted, she felt his lips kiss her ass cheek. "My God, you are driving me wild tonight." A hand squeezed one side of her ass and then just as quickly, his tongue darted into her cheeks and made her entire body go rigid.

What the hell was she allowing to happen? There was no permission asked, simply a passionate young man taking what he was craving. Inhaling deeply, he moaned into her crack and his hands squeezed both halves of her ass without any resistance. She didn't want him to stop. She wanted more.

A low hum came from downstairs with the music playing in the background, but Gabrielle knew she still needed to be quiet. Jordi easily yanked her damp panties aside and then his hot tongue found her slit from behind. Hands massaging her legs and he moaned into her slit while his tongue explored her, and then he sucked one side of her lips and made her moan as well. "Fuck, Gabby…your *poosy* tastes so fucking good."

She was powerless to stop him somehow, her new lover touching her in all the right places. His hands firmly turned her around to face him, and she looked down at the intensity in his face, his tongue darting inside her panties and making her clutch at the sink beside her. All her resolve had been lost, and what she was really craving was for him to lift her up and just slam his massive cock into her and fuck her into oblivion. The intensity of the need she was experiencing had her inhibitions completely destroyed.

Moaning louder, he found her clit and circled it with his tongue tip, making her body sing with pleasure and ripple from top to bottom. Squeezing her thighs around his head, she gasped, having to shove a fist into her mouth to stop from the entire party downstairs hearing her orgasm. Her teeth bit down as the sensations overwhelmed her.

Bucking her hips into his mouth somehow Jordi held onto her hips, letting his tongue dance and take her over the edge to where she threw her head back and gave a silent scream, only a high-pitched squeak escaping her somehow. The shudders overtook her, and she could feel him eagerly lapping away at her inner thighs like he was trying to drink what she had just released.

Once he slowed down, he lifted his head, and his mouth was glistening as he smiled up at her. "You looked so fucking sexy tonight, Gabby. I had to have you. I had to taste you again."

"Jesus. Fuck." She said, gasping for breath. No man had ever brought her to such an intense orgasm in such a short time. He'd been between her legs for maybe a minute, possibly two. Time had stopped.

He stood there grinning, and she saw the bulge in his pants, almost teasing her with the size of it. It would be so easy. Just unzip him, hop up on the counter with her legs spread, and let him fuck her right there. So naughty. So wrong, especially with guests downstairs. And her husband, of course. Sasha would go crazy if she knew.

Her breath was coming in short pants. But just as quickly as he had come into the bathroom, he turned with a wink and slipped back out the bathroom door. Gabrielle felt her legs shaking and turned back to the mirror. Did that really just happen? Within a few minutes the sexy young man had driven her crazy and made her orgasm on his tongue like a freight train.

Once she composed herself and went back downstairs, she absolutely had to confess to somebody what had just happened. Jack wasn't an option, although she resolved that she would definitely tell him as soon as she could.

ere was only one woman she trusted to confess to. Sasha would get a kick out it. Her
st friend was holding court with a couple of guys and seemed to have a steady
eam of wine being poured into her glass. The flirtatious way she held court had
vays made Gabrielle jealous, even though she knew that Sasha craved attention like
 alcoholic craved booze.

rdi was already outside with a couple of his friends, and she could see him talking
d laughing as if nothing had happened upstairs. The only evidence was her flushed
:e and also the dampness still lingering between her legs. And the shaking from the
jasm. She grabbed a glass of wine and downed it in one fast gulp.

sha saw her expression and walked over to her. "Slow down there, hostess.
erything okay?" She looked concerned. At least as concerned as Sasha ever got.

verything's fine. Just need a drink." Gabrielle replied.

ɔoks like you need a bottle." Sasha joked. "What happened?" She glanced down at
ıbrielle's shaking hand.

here's a lot going on, Sash." Gabrielle told her, trying to keep her attention diverted.
t her eyes couldn't help drift over to Jordi, who was looking at her as well. Sasha
ught on right away and grinned.

ɔu know your student can't keep his eyes off you, right? Even though there's about
If a dozen other women trying to get him to fuck them. Including me." Sasha laughed.
e's just got something about him."

efinitely has something about him." Gabrielle agreed, taking another big gulp of wine.
aybe a little bit too much something."

'hat are you talking ab…" Sasha's eyes met hers and she immediately broke out into
nassive grin. "You…you fucking fooled around with him, didn't you? Oh my God!
ıb!" her voice lowered. "Does Jack know? Did he watch like I said?"

ıbrielle looked around. Jack was holding court at the barbecue. She nodded. "He
ows. In fact, we talked about it. Like there's a new agreement in place." Sasha's eyes
ınt wide.

ɔu fucking lucky bitch! So…was it Jordi you decided to play with? It has to be. The
ıy that kid is eye fucking you."

ıbrielle nodded and Sasha stifled another peal of excitement.

ɔu're so fucking lucky. A young stud at home *and* a husband who is okay with it?
sus, my second marriage wouldn't have failed if I had that."

s not so easy, Sash." Gabrielle told her. "It's kind of weird, actually."

ıt…the sex must be amazing?"

Gabrielle couldn't help but look wistful. "We haven't had sex. Yet."

Sasha laughed. "I love how you added a yet to the end of that sentence. But…you mu want to. And Jack? Is he okay with it?"

"I think…he wants to watch it. When we finally do it. And that's a bit weird too. Have y ever?"

She laughed again. "Of course I have. And once you get over the jitters, it's actually really hot. Plus, getting reclaimed…wow."

"What's that?"

"Well, after you're done with your lover, often the partner wants to get in there and sh you who's really the best. Or they like to think they are, anyway. I bet Jack would go wild."

The wine and the orgasm had gotten to Gabrielle's head. "He jerked off on the phone when I told him about it."

"About what, though? What did you do?"

Gabrielle dropped her voice. "We fooled around. Not sex, but…"

"You sucked his dick, didn't you? You just had to see it." When Gabrielle nodded Sas looked around and dropped her voice. "Was it as big as you thought?"

"Bigger." Gabrielle said and Sasha almost squealed. "And he went down on me. Mad me cum so fucking fast."

"And you told Jack afterwards, right? And he was excited?"

"Excited enough to jerk off on the phone."

Sasha let out a loud peal of laughter and then quickly closed it off when others turned see what was going on. Her whisper was still louder than Gabrielle would have liked. told you! He's into it! Now…" she looked around. "You just have to up the ante a bit. [something when he's around, maybe."

Gabrielle laughed. "I guess I just did. Or Jordi did. In the bathroom."

Her eyes went wide. "He…fucked you? Like upstairs?"

"No. But he went down on me sitting on the counter and made me cum again in abou thirty seconds." She almost laughed at herself. It was ridiculous, like something out of porn movie. And it was real. The tingling between her legs told her that.

"Just now? Like that's why you're shaking? Fuck." Sasha frowned. "Damn. And here was thinking I'd take him up there and check out the equipment you told me about. T was if I could drag him away from the young *chicas* he's got clustered around him. Bu okay, he's off limits. All yours, apparently."

ll hers. Those words made Gabrielle's head swim. Jack had no idea that her young
ver had gone down on her better than any man probably ever had right in their master
nsuite. And now, according to their deal, she had to tell him about it.

he rest of the evening seemed to pass in a haze. Gabrielle declined more wine,
ecause she knew getting drunk wasn't a good idea. Her wits needed to be about her
r the inevitable confession to come.

he got everything cleaned up for the most part and thankfully, Jordi went out with his
ends so she and Jack could be alone. Sasha had squeezed her hand before leaving
nd just told her to go for it.

reparing for bed as always, Jack was definitely looking for some sexy time because he
ouldn't keep his hands off her and was trying to kiss her neck repeatedly. Alcohol
ways helped him get amorous. Managing to beat him off and get him to climb into bed,
ne told herself before she left the bathroom that everything was going to be okay. More
an okay, actually.

liding into the sheets next to him, she finally took a deep breath. "So, I think I need to
ll you about something."

ack turned to her and smiled. "You know you can tell me anything."

Earlier in the night, Jordi came into our bathroom with me while I was upstairs alone. A
w hours ago." His eyebrows went up.

Oh yeah? And? Did he make a move on you?"

How do you know I didn't make a move on him?" Gabrielle said with as serious a tone
s she could muster. Jack went quiet, but she could see the wheels turning. "Maybe I
anted him to." She'd already decided that she wanted to tell him, and maybe it could
rn into something as hot as the last time.

Did you? Want him to make a move?" Jack's eyes searched hers. The last time on the
none it hadn't been possible to see his expressions, just hear his voice. Now she could
ee he was actually interested.

he slid her hand under the covers and grabbed Jack's dick, finding that it was already
rowing. "Yes, I did. I wanted him to."

Oh...wow." Jack sighed. "Tell me what happened. Everything."

is cock was getting even harder in her hand by the second. "He came up behind me
nd lifted my dress."

That dress looked fucking amazing on you. I'm not surprised."

He lifted it until I was exposed. He squeezed my bare ass, and I told him to stop, but he
st kept going. He didn't care at all that I told him to stop."

"Uhhh…." Jack's dick flexed and Gabrielle started to slowly stroke him, feeling the length throbbing in her hand. "So, you told him to stop, and he didn't?"

"No. Instead, he got down on his knees and kissed me between my legs. It was so fucking hot. His tongue was between my ass cheeks. And everywhere else."

"He…ate your pussy?" Jack gasped. "From behind? Right in our bathroom?"

"Yes, he did. And it was fucking amazing." Gabrielle leaned down and kissed him, feeling his tongue eagerly enter her mouth. The passion her fulfilled fantasy was creating was something the two of them had never experienced together. "Then he turned me around and licked me everywhere."

"Fuck, Gabby…" Jack moaned. "I don't know why that's making me so hard, but keep talking. Please." His dick was like a steel rod.

Gabrielle needed some satisfaction as well. She slid on top of him. "You know, he mad me cum. So fucking hard." With practiced ease, she grabbed Jack and moved him between her legs, sighing as her husband's familiar member slid into her. There were no panties there on purpose and she was so wet he entered her without any resistanc He groaned as she slid down, her body shuddering.

His eyes looked up into hers. "Did you want to fuck him?"

There was the question floating out between them. It was insane to have her husband inside her and admit something like that, but somehow it felt right to do so. And Gabrielle knew he was okay with knowing about it.

"Yes. I wanted him. We could have fucked right there in the bathroom, and nobody would have ever known." Jack looked up at her and all she saw in his eyes was affection and acceptance.

"You know it's okay, right? It's okay if you want to fuck him." He began to slowly move underneath her and cupped her breasts, but then grabbed her chin. Their lips met, and Gabrielle could feel the affection of what he was doing. He was giving her permission do more than she already had. To liberate her sexual self and give both of them something new in their lives. "If it will make you happy, you can do it."

It almost brought her to tears. The man she loved and had built a life with was telling h that her pleasure, her need was important and that she could fulfill it with his blessing.

"God, you're such an amazing man." Gabrielle sighed. "I'm so lucky." Her hips began t grind up and down on top of him, and the connection she felt between them was intense.

"I think this new arrangement is going to have some serious fringe benefits if this happens when you're turned on." Jack said, as Gabrielle moved her hips faster. She couldn't help herself. There was an itch inside her that Jordi had started earlier and sh needed to scratch it badly. Jack felt good. Good enough, anyway, to give her what she was looking for.

"I bet you wish it was his dick inside you right now." Jack said. Gabrielle's ears perked up. Did that statement mean what she thought it did? Maybe he was interested in hearing how much better endowed her potential new lover was.

"Yes, I do. His dick is so fucking big, baby. I know he'd stretch my pussy right out. So if we fucked afterwards, I'd barely be able to feel you."

"Shit." Jack hissed. "You're so fucking hot. How would you like him to fuck you?" He was thrusting up slowly, but definitely more aggressively than Gabrielle had felt him in a long time. Perhaps their play was a good way for her husband to be fulfilled as well, with some dirty talk that brought an element of humiliation into it. Maybe he truly wanted to be cuckolded.

"I wanted him to lift me up onto the sink earlier and push that massive dick into me. I'd wrap my legs around him and lean back, letting his whole length inside. After all, he'd already made me cum way faster than anyone ever has before, including you. His mouth was fucking amazing. I wanted him to fuck me hard while the entire party listened and cum inside my pussy."

"God, you're so fucking dirty." Jack gasped. "You wanted him to fuck you and then come back downstairs with his cum dripping out of you?"

She decided to take it one step further. "I wanted him to cum in my mouth so I could swallow every drop, and then come downstairs and kiss you."

"Oh, fuck…" Jack pushed up into her harder and Gabrielle put her hands on his chest, squeezing him. It was time to give him a bit of torture. As soon as she saw the familiar quiver in his arms, she stopped moving and he gave out a pathetic mewl underneath her.

"Ah ah…no way you're allowed to cum inside me. I think that little item is going to be reserved for Jordi from now on." She was playing, but his eyes went wide underneath her and he thrashed his head from side to side. He started to beg and it was like music to her ears.

"Please, baby…come on, just let me have one. Let me cum. Please…fuck…" the pleas were just making her even hotter. It was tempting, but Gabrielle knew what she was looking for. A bit of control. In fact, a lot.

"Oh, you can cum." Gabrielle slid off him. "But you're going to cum with your own hand, not my body. At least for a little while until Jordi fills my pussy up." Jack grabbed his rigid dick and began to furiously stroke it as she continued to talk, positioning herself beside him and hissing into his ear. "You're going to watch it, too. Watch him fuck me hard from behind. Hear me scream out every time he makes me cum. And then when he shoots his load inside me, you're going to watch it leak out and maybe I'll even force you to lick it up."

"Fuck! Ahhhhhhh!" Jack gasped loudly and his cock fountained into the air, releasing a thick stream of cream all over his hand and the bed. His hips were spasming and his entire body was rigid as he kept jerking off, draining himself all over their marriage bed to the words Gabrielle was saying.

Just like the reaction he'd had on the phone during their previous talk session, he was panting for breath. Once he was done, his eyes closed, and he dropped his rapidly wilting erection. "Oh my God."

Gabrielle felt so alive. It was an incredible, powerful feeling, confessing to get husband and then being able to tell him what she wanted him to do. A side of things she hadn't even considered. She leaned in and kissed him gently, feeling the breath coming fast and when she touched his chest, his heart was pounding.

A decision was made in that moment, where she knew that the first time she had sex with Jordi was going to be in front of him. Not in a bathroom, not in the woods, but in their marital bed with Jack watching every moment of her surrendering to the young man's massive cock.

It was easy to find the words to support her husband once she had determined what her ultimate plan would be. That she was going to let herself do whatever she and Jordi desired and Jack would submit to being a voyeuristic participant. Whether he liked it or not.

"Good boy."

CHAPTER EIGHT

e next few days passed with no more incidents, and by the time the next weekend led around, Gabrielle had to admit, she was climbing the walls. The sex after she'd nfessed that Jordi made a move on her combined with the submissive way Jack had haved was constantly on her mind, and that was why she decided she needed to test e waters again.

at morning at breakfast she'd invited Jordi to join her for her usual weekend run, and e young man had eagerly accepted. Gabrielle knew a local place they could do some nditioning, and it would also give them a good excuse to be alone together, while ck was at home. Maybe they could have a real conversation about what was ppening without Jack being around.

t it also gave her an idea. A place where the two of them could be alone and maybe ake things physical in more ways than one. The temptation hung over them all and it s becoming hard to ignore,

e you sure you're okay with us going out? I mean…" Gabrielle had intentionally essed herself in a bit more revealing stuff than usual. She was wondering if the fact rdi had become a bit more assertive with seducing her would manifest when they re alone together again.

e sports bra and shorts she wore were usually reserved for a hot yoga studio. The ss backed bra was mostly open in the back and cut perfectly between her breasts. ough support to run in, so nice and tight but also molded to her chest so her ample asts were on display. The shorts were the same colour and just as tight, able to cup r ass cheeks. Because of the tightness she absolutely had to wear a thong, and it ped with ventilation as well.

hink it's a good idea. And damn, babe. That outfit." Jack sighed. "Can't wait until you t home." His eyebrows wiggled.

ure you don't want to join us?" Gabrielle knew he didn't, but she had to ask.

ck slid off the bed and came up behind her as she tugged her shorts into place. ctually…maybe it's a good chance for the two of you to be alone?"

ddenly, she realized what he was saying. And that even though he knew fully that rdi might make a move on her and she might accept, he was going to wait at home her to come back and tell him about it. "Are you saying what I think you're saying? u mean, if I want to…"

ou definitely can. Whatever happens, happens. I just want to hear about it when you t home." Jack said, wrapping his arms around her from behind. The incredible thing s Gabrielle could feel he was semi-hard pressing into her.

She felt a surge of affection and turned around, pulling his head towards her and kissi him hard. They made out furiously like teenagers as Jack groped at her ass, a thrill passing through her body that she was about to head out to be alone with Jordi and g sweaty. When they broke off the kiss, Jack simply kissed her forehead. "I love you."

"I love you too." Gabrielle sighed. She pushed him away and readjusted her shorts an sports bra as Jordi's bedroom door opened.

He was wearing shorts as well, and Gabrielle knew he must have been wearing some pretty incredibly tight underwear, otherwise his long penis would be dangling out. The tank top showed off his sculpted arms.

He walked into the doorway and when he saw Gabrielle, he eyed her up and down wi a lascivious look, then glanced over at Jack, who returned his look with a smile.

"She looks good, doesn't she?" her husband said. Jordi looked slightly surprised and then recovered quickly, smiling and nodding with flushed cheeks. "You two have a go time working out. I'm going to enjoy my morning playing video games."

Gabrielle almost felt nervous. It was like she was being sent away on a date with another man, even though a run and a workout seemed innocent enough. "Let's go. I about two miles to the outdoor area and then we can either walk or run back when we done."

"*Bueno.*" Jordi said. Once they were outside and she warmed up a bit, Gabrielle took towards the area she was thinking about. It was a cool morning, but her body quickly warmed up and Jordi had no problem keeping up with her stride.

"We can head over here, through the trail." There was an extensive outdoor path system where they lived, and many people took advantage of it, especially on weeker mornings. That was the only issue Gabrielle could see. There was no way Jordi woulc make a move on her if there were other people around.

Once they arrived at the outdoor workout area, she was happy there was nobody else around. It gave her some opportunity to flirt a bit. Although she didn't even have to, Jordi was flirting enough for both of them combined. Smiling at her and touching her a every opportunity.

When they went to perform some pull-ups, he confidently placed his hands on her bar waist and lifted her like a feather. When she dropped to the ground, he grabbed her around the waist, and she could feel he was already semi-hard under his shorts.

Gabrielle did lots of bending exercises to show off her booty, which he was definitely appreciating. Normally, she would have hated a man leering at her ass while she worked out, which happened sometimes at the gym, but this was different. The smoldering sexual tension between them was unspoken, but definitely permeated the surrounding air.

nother trainer suddenly emerged from the woods with a group of four women and arted putting them through circuits. Their alone time was gone. Gabrielle decided she ad to make a move to get them somewhere else, where maybe they could indulge eir obvious needs.

et's head this way. It loops around by the path and then heads back." Jordi nodded, a ght sheen of sweat coating his chest and arms. He looked absolutely delicious. hroughout the workout, he'd been lifting his shirt to wipe the sweat off him, showing er his chiseled stomach.

ney jogged down the path and suddenly Jordi grabbed her by the wrist, almost yanking er down a secluded trail into an area that was surrounded by trees and dense vergrowth. Nobody would have seen it unless they looked hard.

s soon as they were alone, Gabrielle began to talk but before she could even open her outh, Jordi had her pushed up against one of the trees and his mouth was on hers, ssing her with intense passion.

er body went tense and then she relaxed into the kiss, enjoying the fact his firm body as pressing against her and she could feel his hard cock against her bare thigh. Her pples hardened instantly, and she suddenly wished she was completely bare under er shorts. Somehow the young man had her ready to go within seconds.

Ve are alone, Gabby. And I want you. You are so fucking gorgeous." He sighed, his ngue sliding up her sweaty neck and his hands cupping her breasts through the sports a. Sliding his hands up, he pushed her straps aside with ease and suddenly her easts were free in the air as she gasped with surprise.

was slightly cold outside, and her nipples were rock hard from being exposed. As oon as Jordi's tongue licked one of her tips, she hissed with the sensation. It was warm nd cold at the same time and goosebumps were running up and down her flesh. by...you are so fucking *sexy.*" he sighed. Sucking her breast lightly, he nipped her pple right at the tip and made her pulse with need.

nd she *felt* sexy. This young man who was completely seducing her was making her el desired, younger, even completely uninhibited. After all, she was standing in a rest against a tree and his lips and hands were all over her.

iding a hand under her waistband, he kissed her hard and with no hesitation, suddenly er drenched panties were shoved aside and a finger entered her dripping tunnel. h...oh...fuck..." she sighed. His fingertip spread around the lubricant that her body as emitting, and she suspected what he had in mind. He wanted her and he wasn't ing to be denied.

nere was definitely no stopping the freight train, and Jordi seemed to not care at all hen a bicycle skated by quickly, only a dozen meters away. Gabrielle looked over as e man looked over and quickly grinned, and then turned to ride away, leaving them to their somewhat public moment. Jordi didn't stop kissing her neck and her breasts, and when another finger entered her, Gabrielle gasped again. Her hand groped down for h crotch and found that he was hard as a rock.

His eyes met hers with intensity. "You want that? It's so fucking hard. See what you do to me, Gabby?"

"Oh my God, Jordi." Gabrielle sighed. "You are driving me crazy." The fingers continue to move inside her, and it was impossible to turn back. It was past the point of no retur and the entire morning had led up to what she was about to allow her sexy young student to do to her. Turning around, she slid her shorts down further and bent over. " want you inside me."

"Oh my God…" Jordi moaned, and his hands squeezed her ass cheeks, separating them as Gabrielle felt her pussy lips open with a wet sensation. She was more than ready to receive him, even though he was easily going to be the biggest man she had ever experienced. He pulled down his shorts and stepped behind her, and as he did, she felt his gigantic cock head rub up and down her wet slit from behind.

But it couldn't happen. The first time she let him fuck her she wanted Jack to see it. Fo him to be a part of it. For him to give her the all clear and then support her accepting another man inside her.

"Wait." Somehow she found her senses and get some clarity, even though she'd just invited him to bend her over. Having Jordi fuck her in the woods wasn't the way she wanted to experience him for the first time. Even though having his gigantic dick about to penetrate her was almost too much to resist. "We can't. Not here."

Even though she knew he was desperate to enjoy her, Jordi stepped back and pulled up her shorts as if creating a barrier that he wouldn't be able to penetrate. He grabbed her and spun her around, kissing her hard again. As her bare back scratched against the rough bark, Gabrielle felt a passion she'd never felt before.

True lust, wanting, and she knew that the first they were going to really be together would be absolutely explosive. But it was something she wanted to share with Jack. H husband.

"There's something I want from you." She declared. After all, just because she wasn't going to let him fuck her didn't mean she didn't want to pleasure him. And maybe there was a way to involve Jack somehow. Her mind raced into a scenario that she couldn't resist.

Her hand found his massive erection and, while rubbing it, his lips were on her neck again. Licking, sucking and driving her crazy.

"*Que es eso?*" Jordi said, grabbing the sides of his shorts and tugging them down. Suddenly his massive dick was exposed in her hand, and Gabrielle wrapped her finge around the thick shaft, feeling him pulsing hot in her palm, freely open in the air. "*Queres eso?*" *You want that?*

"Yes…" Gabrielle licked her lips. She felt complete freedom. The entire forest had stilled around them, and she couldn't believe it was even her body about to do what she had suddenly thought of. "I want that. Between these." Her hand ran between her breasts. Beginning to stroke him slowly, she crouched down and lifted one of her breasts. "I want you to cum all over me."

Jordi hissed and reached out to brace himself against the tree. "Ai…fuck…" Gabrielle knew from the way he was throbbing in her hand it wasn't likely to take long. Her hand sped up, and she couldn't resist dipping her mouth down and letting her tongue slide across the top of the head of his cock. He moaned and his cock flexed in her hand.

Like she had the first time, she placed his big dick between her breasts and felt the heat of him rubbing up and down the centre, trying to let him feel her velvet skin squeezing his dick as much as possible. At the base, she held him and played with his balls.

Pumping between her breasts, Jordi looked intensely ferocious, almost as if he wanted to devour her. With the expression on his face, Gabrielle was surprised he didn't just try to throw her down and mount her like two rutting animals. He was getting closer by the second to giving her what she wanted.

Faster. Her hand got into a steady rhythm, and she could feel his body responding. He began to pulse and give out quick gasps of breath. Gabrielle pointed his massive cock at her bare breasts and was rewarded when a thick stream of white shot out and coated the bare, sweaty skin. Continuing to tug on him, he kept spurting until her breasts were thoroughly covered and his thick seed was dripping off her nipples, down to her bare stomach.

"*Dios mio,* Gabby." Jordi panted while looking down at her, and his dick continued to have small drops released from the end. Even though her body was already covered and she was exhilarated, she couldn't resist popping the head into her lips and sucking gently, tasting the salty flavour of him and enjoying his hiss of sensitivity.

Licking her lips, she ran her hand across her chest and enjoyed the fact his cum was rubbing all over her skin. It coated her quickly like lotion, and as Jordi tucked his deflating cock back into his shorts, she looked around.

Nobody was the wiser what had happened in their secluded pocket of the woods, but there was a group of walkers coming down the trail. She tugged up her sports bra to cover her sticky chest. "We should get going."

Jordi nodded with his typical grin and then followed her, walking out of the treed area with his eyes still boring holes in her tight shorts. Once they were back on the trail, without a word, Gabrielle broke into a run. The thrill of what had happened gave her adrenaline, and she was eager to get home to see Jack after what had happened. They jogged into the driveway and Jordi's hands went to his knees, panting for breath. "Thank you for the workout." Was all he said with a wink.

She could tell he wanted to embrace her, but not in the middle of their very public driveway. After all, he'd had just as much fun as she had. But the last piece of the puzzle was still there to be put in. Actually having sex with each other.

In the meantime, she needed to fulfill Jack's part of the arrangement, and she was definitely horny enough to need to take care of that as soon as possible.

Jack stood in the kitchen alcove when they stepped inside. "So, how was the run?" It seemed somehow perfectly normal that he was greeting his wife and their young student after what had essentially been a date. And he had no idea how close it came to being even more. "You guys have fun?" Her flushed face could have easily been from the workout, but Gabrielle knew it was much more.

"Very much fun." Jordi said with a smile. "Gabrielle is an excellent runner. She is very strong as well." Gabrielle giggled. Jack was looking her up and down, as if trying to figure out more details. She knew her hair was wild.

"He tired me out. I haven't worked that hard in a while." Gabrielle joked. "I'm going to get changed." Jack nodded. Jordi smiled at her and then she walked up the stairs to the bedroom, hearing Jordi's door close not long after.

Within moments, it seemed, Jack was knocking on the bathroom door as she was washing her face with an expression like he was a child waiting for Christmas.

"So? It was fun?" The undertone of the question was obvious.

"It was really fun." She said, nodding in the mirror. "Just give me a minute and I'll catch you up." He nodded and returned to the bedroom. Looking at herself in the mirror, Gabrielle couldn't hide what had happened. He deserved to know, and maybe she could get some enjoyment out of telling him. After the last time, she knew Jack was definitely into her telling him about what happened.

Sliding off her sports bra, she let it drop to the floor and then slid her shorts down as well. A reminder as she stood there naked of how close she had been to letting Jordi do...well, what she really wanted him to do. And maybe what Jack would let happen.

She just had to feel like she had permission to take it that ultimate step and she hoped that after what she was about to tell him, he would give her what she was craving.

Jack was sitting on the bed when she walked back into the bedroom wearing only her panties. She could hear the shower running in the spare bathroom, so for the time being, Jordi was occupied.

Gabrielle approached him, sidling up to the bed and letting her sticky breasts sway. He looked her up and down and sighed. "Goddamn you're gorgeous. I hope you had a good time."

ke I said, it was fun." Gabrielle felt every bit the seductress and climbed onto his lap, addling him and kissing him deeply with her tongue sliding across his lips. She was anely horny, and she could feel Jack hard underneath his pants already, just from sing her.

ey made out, his hands finding her breasts and teasing her nipples and massaging r naked thighs. "And yes, in case you were wondering. We fooled around."

id he have his hands all over you?" He ran his hand down her long legs. Gabrielle shed. "I bet he wanted to do this."

e did. He touched me. A lot." She offered, and Jack leaned in to kiss her again.

o…what happened? Tell me." He looked her in the eye, and Gabrielle knew she was idy to describe everything that had happened between them. She stood up and itioned him back onto the bed.

ake off your pants first." Gabrielle commanded. Easily, he skimmed off his clothing d his cock popped into view. Knowing what Jordi was sporting made his dick almost k small, but she knew it wasn't. Just average. It had always been enough, at least til now. But it was definitely hard. She climbed onto the bed and knelt beside him.

id you get in a good workout? I mean, is he in good shape?" He sounded like an ger puppy.

e's strong for his size." Her hands trailed up Jack's chest. "And we did a lot of spotting ch other. I enjoyed touching his muscles. He's ripped."

ounded slightly like he was making a suggestion. "Was he…touching you? Flirting?"

g time." Gabrielle laughed. "I mean, it's part of the workout, but he was definitely ng it to his advantage. His hands were all over my ass. My legs."

id did that…get you excited?" His hand squeezed her thigh, and Gabrielle felt a rge of desire. Her nipples pebbled with the excitement of telling someone what had ppened. "Did you get…turned on?"

ially, she could nod. "Yes. I did." Jack's cock twitched, and Gabrielle let her hand drift vards it, running her fingertips across his thighs and up his hips. Jack twitched derneath her touch and his dick shivered. "I got insanely turned on. And then he ggested we head further down the trail, where it was more secluded."

looked into her eyes and nodded. "I know what that means. Did he make a move?"

brielle sighed. "We were alone. He grabbed me and kissed me. Hard. And he was y making out with me. I didn't stop him." Her mouth was dry.

ck's hand found hers and with a surprising movement, he placed her hand on his ection. She wrapped her hand around it and he moaned in his throat.

"How long did you make out for?" he croaked.

"A while. He was touching me, too. Playing with my breasts. Teasing my nipples. He had me pinned against a tree." She began to slowly stroke her husband, letting her hand give just enough grip to make him feel it. Every couple of strokes, she would sw her hand around his head, and he thrust with his hips. "He got my bra down and suck on my nipples."

"Jesus." Jack moaned again. "That's so fucking hot, babe. Right there in the open?"

She nodded. "I couldn't believe it was happening. But it felt…fantastic."

"So…what happened then?"

"I was this close to letting him fuck me. Right there in the woods." Gabrielle confesse "I was so fucking turned on, babe. He was playing with me and kissing me…and…"

She could see that Jack's mind was processing what she had just said, but she want to make sure that he didn't think for one second she hadn't thought about the consequences of what had almost happened.

Leaning down, she took his rigid erection into her lips and sucked gently, then ran he tongue down the edge of his cock with a moan. "You can't imagine how wet I was. H much I was craving getting fucked like a slut right there in the open where people cou walk by and see us."

"But you didn't."

"No." Gabrielle looked into his eyes. "The first time I fuck him you're going to watch u Jack closed his eyes, a shudder passing through his body. Like he was admitting to himself what was inevitably going to happen.

Finally, he opened his eyes and asked, "So he was fingering you?"

Gabrielle sighed. "With two fingers. He made me cum all over his hand. It only took a minute or two because I was so horny."

"But you didn't let him fuck you?" Like he needed to confirm it.

"No…" she paused. "But I jerked him off. And…" she grabbed Jack's hand and place on her naked chest. "He came all over my tits."

His eyes went wide, and she saw his cock jerk. "Oh my God…" the moan was almos sensual. "You mean these were covered with his cum?"

"I wiped it all over them just for you. All over my naked skin. Now, I want you to taste

Leaning forward to offer him her bare breasts, she saw Jack hesitate and then his lip kissed one. Gabrielle sighed with satisfaction. "That's good, baby. Now lick them. I w you to lick them all over."

uuuck." Jack growled, but then his tongue started to skate across her naked skin as abrielle played with his rock hard dick. He seemed to give in and relax and suddenly s hands were pushing her breasts together as he used his tongue all over her globes, asing her erect nipples at the same time. "You taste fucking amazing, baby."

roking his hair, Gabrielle encouraged him. "See? It feels good, doesn't it?" Jack oked up at her with child-like eyes and nodded. She pulled him up, and they kissed ard, tongues wrestling in each others' mouths. It was making Gabrielle crazy.

ropping her head down, she licked the tip of his erection and then engulfed the first uple of inches with her mouth. Sucking him gently, Gabrielle enjoyed her husband eing pleasured after hearing about her fun with her new lover.

ick moaned again but stroked her hair at the same time. "So, you definitely want to ck him?"

ie sucked her husband into her mouth again. "Yes. I want to fuck him. I want to know nat that dick feels like. I want to cum all over it." Licking his shaft, she dipped her head id ran her tongue across his balls as he groaned again, tightening his other hand on e sheets. "Just like I want to cum all over this right now."

iet on top of me." Jack commanded. Gabrielle scrambled up and mounted him, and nen she felt how hard he was, a sharp hiss escaped her while his cock easily slid all e way to the hilt into her dripping wet hole as she sank down.

'eeeesssss…" Gabrielle sighed. She knew she didn't have to be quiet either, and likely eir exchange student was listening in and maybe even stroking his cock, listening to ir. "That's so good, baby. I need this dick."

iut you want his dick, don't you? You wish you were fucking him instead of me." Jack owled underneath her. Gabrielle looked down and saw a twinkle in his eye. There was omething there that it was easy to tell he wanted to explore.

aybe it was time to see if her husband was into a bit of humiliation and might enjoy earing about how much she was craving her new young lover. Or soon to be lover.

le's just so fucking big. I can tell when he puts it inside me it would stretch me so wide. o much bigger than your dick. I want to get stretched out like that." Gabrielle ground ir hips down as she spoke and could feel Jack's cock perfectly, but she knew if she as doing the same thing to Jordi he would rub against her deepest walls. "If I was on p of him, I don't think it would even fit. I'd be so fucking full."

ie felt him swell inside her and the sensations were the same as they always had een. Pleasurable. Jack was a great lover; he just wasn't the grab you by the hair and ck you in a forest type of lover. He had what her girlfriends referred to as "boyfriend ck". And that was fine.

Thinking about Jordi and talking about it was making her want something. A little more "If he fucked me and then I put your cock in, I bet I'd barely feel it. He would stretch m out so much he'd ruin me for all other men."

"Fuuuuuccckk..." Jack began thrusting harder. "You wouldn't be satisfied with me anymore?"

Gabrielle stopped her motion and squeezed her kegel muscles. There was a very erot element to being in control, and while their sex was always good, having him almost begging her underneath her and controlling everything that they were doing was sending it to another level. Especially talking about her taking another lover. A young lover. A really, really well endowed lover.

"Once I had his dick, this would feel so small. I don't think you'd be able to satisfy me anymore. I'd have to keep finding massive cocks to fuck just to have an orgasm."

"You'd be my big cock hotwife slut." Jack grabbed her hips and, with no warning, flippe them both over. There was a look in his eye that Gabrielle hadn't seen before. Something almost primal. He threw her down and mounted her from behind, and she gasped as he slid into the hilt with one hard thrust, beginning to fuck her hard and fast without holding back.

Usually, he made sure she came first, but what they were doing was spurring him towards something selfish. And it was insanely hot. "My dirty little hotwife looking for strange dick and getting fucked while I'm away."

Oh, is that what you want? "Just imagine coming home and hearing me crying out in this bed because another man is fucking me so hard and I'm cumming. You'd have t walk in and watch me begging him for more!"

Jack was slamming into her from behind, squeezing her ass cheeks and driving his cock into her with rapid beats against the bedsheets. Gabrielle felt her body building towards something massive. "Don't stop!" she cried. "Fuck me like you want to watch another man fuck me!"

He grabbed her hair and yanked her head back, Gabrielle letting go with a massive cr of delight at the way he was manhandling her. Like another man had possessed him. His cock continued to ravage her pussy hard and deep, and suddenly she felt herself peaking and gave a loud gasp as she put her head down and her pussy clenched ontc his thrusting member.

With a last gasp Jack drove into her one more time and she felt him spurt a massive load of heat into her eager tunnel, his hips bucking against her with every beat and fle. of him emptying inside. When he was done moving, he collapsed on her back and kissed her between the shoulder blades as his softening cock slid out of her pussy. A deep groan came from his throat. "Holy...shit..."

Gabrielle collapsed onto her stomach, feeling her pussy oozing out the massive load her husband had just pumped into her. She was breathing in short pants and couldn't remember the last time they'd had sex that good. So primal, so intense. It was exactly what she was hoping for when she had thought about entertaining the notion of another man being involved in their sex life.

Groaning, she slid sideways, and Jack wrapped his arms around her, lovingly cradling her into his naked chest. The way he was so loving about what they were doing made her feel a warm flush of acceptance and affection, and she kissed his chest gently. "Wow."

"Yeah. Wow." Jack agreed. "That was amazing." She kissed his chest again.

The unspoken words were that it was so amazing because of what they had been talking about. Because of her fooling around in the woods with their young student and then having her come home horny and ready for her husband to enjoy her.

There they were, both knowing that their sex life had been given new life by a scenario that most couples would have avoided at all costs.

She hadn't even noticed that they left the door open, but there it was slightly ajar, and it would have been impossible for Jordi not to hear what they were doing right after the two of them fooled around in the woods. The shower had likely stopped running a while before they finished.

Did Jordi hear them? Gabrielle hoped so, because it meant that he would know that the sex she and Jack had was insanely hot right after they had fooled around in the woods. All she had to do was set the right scene and then the last bit of her seduction could fall into place. And she could finally get what she had been building towards for weeks. Her young stud being able to enjoy every inch of each other while her husband watched.

CHAPTER NINE

Somehow, all three of them restrained themselves for a couple of days, but Gabrielle had made sure that she wasn't alone with Jordi without Jack being around. It was on her mind constantly, but she also knew that Jack had to be the one to give the green light for what was naturally going to happen next between the three of them. And she didn't even have to wait until he went away.

Jordi's exchange session was ending, and it meant that an ideal scenario was about to come into play. Gabrielle could indulge her fantasy and then he would fly home, likely never to be seen again. And she and Jack could figure out how they wanted their relationship to grow afterwards without the tension of a lover under the same roof.

It also gave them a timeline. She had to make herself available. If she did, it was guaranteed that Jordi would take advantage of it. Finally, the right situation came about.

Gabrielle told Jack to stay late at the office, and she was going to pretend that she was frustrated about it when she got home. She hoped that would spur her young lover to attempt to enjoy her before her husband returned home, and then she could contact Jack and make sure he was home for the event they were all looking forward to.

Walking into their home the next evening, she saw Jordi studying again in the living room. He looked up, and Gabrielle put on the act she'd spoken to Jack about. "God, that's so frustrating!" she dropped her bag roughly on the ground and Jordi stood up, looking concerned.

"Is everything okay, Gabby? You look *muy molesta.*"

"I'm fine. Just…I hate feeling alone all the time." She saw his eyes perk up and then, as if wheels were turning in his head, he stepped forward as she continued. "Jack…Mr. Richards has to work late again. I have no idea when he'll be home. I guess it's just the two of us."

Jordi grinned. "I would enjoy that. Perhaps we can have dinner together?"

Gabrielle smiled in return. "I think that's a great idea. Maybe we order in? I can open a bottle of wine." She knew she was likely to need some liquid courage. He nodded in response, and she saw him step closer.

"I am so grateful that we have gotten to know each other, you know." He offered. "I think you are a wonderful woman, and Mister Richards doesn't know what he has waiting for him at home."

Walking forward, she extended her arms and hugged the young man, feeling his arms wrap around her tightly. Intentionally, she looked into his eyes, and let the sexual tension between them build a bit, almost as if it was a tease. Jordi looked already as if wanted to devour her, and Gabrielle knew if she kept it up he'd likely literally tear her thes off at some point. Stepping back, she sighed. "I'll order some food and open a ttle."

nodded, and she walked into the kitchen, pulling up Uber Eats and ordering them a e Spanish themed meal. When she walked back out into the living room with a wine ttle and two glasses, Jordi snapped his book shut and sat back on the couch. Pouring m two glasses, she offered a toast. "To your last couple of days here."

thout a word, he took a sip and put his glass down, blatantly sliding his eyes ductively up her bare thigh. Gabrielle had chosen her dress carefully to be something rk worthy, but just tight and revealing enough.

e wanted to tease him. She wanted him to crave her, to want to tear her clothes off, t still control things just like she had with Jack when she made him hold off on his gasm. Every part of her knew that eventually she'd have her sexy young man in her lm. And her mouth and pussy.

ou know, I never expected to meet a woman like you." Jordi said. "When my other ends told me about their experiences, they were so…how you say…vanilla?" He slid en closer to her, so their thighs were touching. "You have made this time here so azing for me. I need to thank you."

brielle took another sip of her wine. "I think you've already thanked me a couple of es." She gave him a wink, and he laughed. "And I'm hoping maybe you can thank me e more time."

vould love that." Jordi said. "Right now." He leaned in and when their lips met, it was an electric shock rolled through Gabrielle's body. It was sensual, the way he nibbled her lips and his tongue gently probed her mouth while his hand slid up her dress with hesitation. When his fingers touched her damp panties, Gabrielle moaned into his ger mouth.

king out with even more passion, he plunged his hands into her hair and then began gently push her back on the couch, but before they could keep going, the doorbell ng, making both of them startle. Jordi sat up and looked at the door. "That must be the d." Gabrielle pushed him away and, with a smile, strutted to the door.

e delivery man had a big smile on his face once she opened the door, and once the d was in her hands, she moved to the kitchen, Jordi trailing behind like an obedient p. She turned to him as he stepped closer. "I think we should eat before this gets d. We have lots of time."

nodded, confidently knowing that seducing her was only a matter of time, and ened the cutlery drawer as she prepared two plates and then poured them both some re wine. The food was excellent as always, and even just talking to a young man o was so enamored with her was completely comfortable. Gabrielle realized she was probably going to miss having the young stud around the house, especially with the fringe benefits that had become part of his stay. Having him leaving also brought a few questions along with it, namely how were she and Jack supposed to move forward on the primary object of her desire was gone?

It felt intimate, and Jordi was flirting with her in every movement of his eyes and body. Gabrielle definitely wasn't denying his sexual energy, and by the time they got up to clear the dishes, it was impossible to deny what was going on between them.

She closed the dishwasher and then turned around, and Jordi was looming over her. close as he could be without actually touching her. The sexual energy between them like it was cutting off her breath.

"I'm sorry, Gabby. I can't stop thinking about your body. Your lips. Your breasts. Your sexy ass." He stepped closer and the heat between them became a raging inferno.

"Oh, my." Gabrielle was trying to be coy, but it was impossible. She had a green light do whatever she pleased, and now it was finally time to enjoy her sexy young man wi every inch of her body. "Jordi, we can't…" It was hard to stifle a giggle because she knew she wasn't going to stop him but had to play the game.

"We can. Mr. Richards isn't here. We can enjoy each other for a long time." His head leaned in, and he kissed her neck. Any resolve she might have had towards stopping him crumbled away and when his lips found hers, she allowed his tongue into her mo and sucked on it gently.

Grabbing her hair, he turned her around and pressed his massive hardness into her. Gabrielle felt like she was being deliciously seduced by an expert lover.

His hands cupped her breasts from behind, and he knew exactly the right way to let h fingertips slide across her nipples. Lips on her neck were hot and sent a searing ripple of pleasure up her spine. "*Dios mio.* You are so *fucking* sexy." He sighed into her ear. want you, Gabrielle. I want to consume you."

Jesus. Just the way he was being so passionate was driving her wild. Without waiting for an answer, he spun her around and then his hands were squeezing her breasts again and massaging them while he kissed her neck from the front and let his mouth trail down between them. "These are *muy increible.* I must have them."

Even though he was young, the guy had moves that could get women's panties off in moments, even if she hadn't already let him. Like during their outdoor workout, if she didn't stop what was happening and slow things down, Jack was going to walk into the house and be able to catch the two of them fucking in the living room. Without him.

She stroked his hair and looked into his eyes. "Let's wait. Just until Mr. Richards gets home. I just have to text him and he will come."

s eyebrows flew up. "*Que?* What do you mean? He is not gone?" Jordi was searching
er eyes. "How…" then the realization dawned on his face. "Ahhh…*lo entiendo.* He
ants to…join us?"

le wants to watch us." Gabrielle finally admitted, her face blushing. A big smile broke
ut over Jordi's face. He nodded and then leaned in to kiss her neck gently again.

would love that." He said simply. "If it means I get to pleasure you properly. After all,
e should be a part of it. If he will enjoy watching me with you, then…"

abrielle's head was spinning. It wasn't exactly the reaction she was expecting, but it
as actually the one she was hoping for. All three of them on the same page together
nd able to just come out and admit what they truly wanted. She wanted Jordi. Jordi
anted her. And Jack wanted to be there to watch her be enjoyed. "I'll text him and tell
m to come home." Jordi nodded as Gabrielle grabbed her phone.

ome home. We are ready.

I be there soon.

ne response came quickly, and suddenly Gabrielle was nervous. Now all the pressure
as off. Sort of. Now it was just a matter of finding out if she was not only comfortable
tting another man finally have sex with her, but also if Jack was going to be okay with
itnessing it.

m going to get changed. And when Mr. Richards comes home, we can have some
n. *Entender?"*

i." Jordi grinned. He kissed her again, hard, and Gabrielle's legs almost buckled. She
uld feel his massive cock pressing into her thigh and now that she knew she was
ing to enjoy it, she wanted it as soon as possible inside her. "I can wait. But him…" he
abbed her hand and Gabrielle felt him hard and eager underneath. "…he can't wait
ng."

ne texted Jack quickly. **When you get home, just come upstairs.**

on't do anything with him until I get there.

ne response took her breath away. He'd accepted that he was going to watch his wife
ith another man and was just asking her to hold off. Which was going to be hard
nough, considering how intensely wet her pussy was already and how hard Jordi was.

ne turned to Jordi. "Come upstairs in ten minutes." Gabrielle knew that would give
ack enough time to get home since he wasn't far away and allow her to get ready. The
ntire environment had to be perfect for the first time she'd allow herself to have another
an inside her while someone watched.

ntering her bedroom, she had the lingerie she had planned to wear already picked out.
gainst her darker skin, white lingerie always made Jack crazy, and there was one

particular set that he always virtually tore off her because it looked exotic and contrasted her glow perfectly. The bra was lacy and a demi cup that supported her, but also left her nipples seen through the thin material, ready to be touched. The panties were high on her waist and almost sheer as well, with a lovely fringe of lace around them and a thong back that pulled directly up her ass cheeks. The completion of the package was the stockings, also white and sheer.

Tugging the stockings up her long legs she could feel the delicate material hugging her and the panties cupping her engorged mound just reinforced that she was eager to be touched there. It was fun to feel sexy, and especially fun to feel sexy knowing that Jordi was going to enjoy it along with Jack.

Just putting it all on made her buzz with anticipation, and when she touched up her makeup and brushed out her hair, it made her realize how long it had been since she really put some effort into looking sexy for her husband. And here she was, doing it for another lover.

Lighting some candles for the mood, she heard Jordi climbing the stairs and when he walked into the bedroom, his shirt was stripped off quickly. Even though she knew she should wait for Jack, Gabrielle didn't deny him when he quickly crossed to her and kissed her with passion, his hands immediately squeezing her bare ass and feeling like he was touching everywhere at once. Even just making out with him was so incredible.

They broke the kiss when a noise from downstairs alerted them both that her husband had arrived, and frustratingly slowly, Jack came up the stairs and then tentatively entered the bedroom, immediately seeing Jordi with his shirt off and Gabrielle in her lingerie. In the candlelight she could see how awestruck he was, even though he was nervous.

"Wow. You look incredible, babe." Jordi voluntarily stood off to the side, nonplussed that her husband had entered the room. His cock was at full mast already, bound under his pants, but it was obvious how thick and long he was.

Knowing she needed to make sure he was ready, Gabrielle walked to Jack and kissed him softly. "I hope this is okay." She pointed to the chair in the corner she'd set up intentionally for him to watch from. "I want everything to be for both of us."

Without a word, Jack walked to the chair and sat down, looking at both of them and she could see the conflict in his eyes. He was as unsure as he was at how he was supposed to feel or react to another man standing there shirtless, about to fuck his wife.

Gabrielle knew she had to control things. Take the lead and just go with the faith that her husband would be okay with what was happening.

She looked at Jordi. "Lie down. Make sure he can see you. Take everything off." The young man slid onto the bed and undid his pants, quickly sliding them off along with his underwear. The massive dick she adored came slowly into view, and just like the first time she saw it, the size took Gabrielle's breath away. Long and sticking straight up, the shaft pulsed with need and had one tantalizing drop of precum at the head. Just seeing it again made her shiver.

Moving herself onto the bed, she slid across Jordi's body and kissed him, wanting to make sure that the moment felt intimate for her young lover as well. He ran his hands down her bare waist and then skated a hand up to tease her nipples.

With practiced skill he undid her bra and Gabrielle let it fall away, turning to Jack to show him her naked breasts. His expression was rapt on her and he smiled to reassure her so far he was okay.

Turning her head, she bobbed and ran her tongue down the side of Jordi's shaft, marveling at the fact it was so incredibly hard for her. He stroked her hair softly as she ran her tongue up and down and then finally slipped her mouth over the head, sucking gently. Rewarded with a loud moan, she heard a moan come from the other side of the room from her watching husband as well.

"Look at his dick, baby. It's so big." She held it in her hand and placed it against her cheek so that Jack could easily see how gigantic Jordi was from across the room. Licking the tip quickly, she heard Jordi take a sharp breath in and when she wrapped her lips around his thick head he moaned, arching his back. "And he tastes so good."

Finally her husband spoke. "He's stretching your mouth out, isn't he?" Jack said. "I can see it."

"It's hard to get it all inside." Gabrielle slid her mouth over his spongy head and then went down a couple of inches, making Jordi's cock hit the back of her throat and giving out a large gasp. Moving quickly up and down, the low sound of her sucking echoed in the room between them. It was glorious. And she was intentionally making the sound more audible with every lick and suck to make sure Jack could hear it.

Her lover began to get into it and started to flex his hips, driving his cock up into her eager mouth as she consumed him with delight. Her panties were drenched with desire. Angling her ass towards her husband, she turned onto her side and pulled her legs up to show Jack her wet slit while Jordi got onto his knees and stroked her hair, slipping his dick between her lips and beginning to fuck her mouth.

Like she thought a porn star might, Gabrielle moaned with every thrust of the massive cock slamming into her lips and throat, and her words spilled out when she could take a breath, giving her husband a play-by-play of exactly how she was feeling.

"Ah…ah…fuck…he's fucking my lips so hard…yes…I love it, babe…his big dick is stretching my mouth…" Gasps and choking sounds intermingled with her lusty words.

"Fuuuuck…" she heard Jack sigh but wasn't even looking towards him. The cock slamming between her lips was bordering on that thin line between pleasure and pain, and it was thrilling. Jordi was fucking her mouth with vigor, and all she could think of was that she wanted to finally feel it in her pussy, filling her and stretching her like she'd never felt before.

His cock released from her mouth with a loud slurp and a gasp, and Gabrielle scrambled onto the bed. "Fuck me. Fuck me hard!" She gasped. Jordi lined himself up between her legs, grabbing her thighs and easily positioning her so that his massive dick was placed between her legs. But he paused again.

"Mira eso? Te voy a follar ahora." He said. *See that? I'm going to fuck you.* Telling her what he was going to do but then holding back and running his cock head up and down her dripping wet slit almost made her plead for him to slip it inside her. His head teased her clit, and she ground her hips.

"Por favor…por favor…si…" she asked him please, and finally his massive head split her lips and he pushed inside, making her entire body go wild. The intense pressure of his thickness splitting her open and the length that he thrust inside with one simple movement was more than she ever thought she could take. "FUUUUCKKKK!" Gabrielle cried. "Fuck meeeeee….yeeessss…!"

Jordi pumped between her legs quickly without hesitating, his balls slapping against her ass while his cock plumbed her deepest depths. He had just as much need for satisfaction as she did. Claiming her hard and deep like he had likely been craving ever since she was with him the first time on the couch.

The size and the intensity of him sent her over the orgasmic edge almost immediately and Gabrielle realized she was about to cum after only moments, wrapping her legs around him and wailing with intense screams of passion. He growled over her, relentless in his assault on her pussy. There was no end to his movements, and his muscles flexed above her while he fucked her like nobody ever had before.

His stamina was like nothing she'd ever experienced. There was no way with the steady pace of his cock inside her that Jack or any other man would have lasted more than a minute, but Jordi could control every part of what he was doing to her body.

He squeezed her breasts and when he found her clit with his hand, easily taking one leg over his shoulder, he made her cum again with a loud wail, her pussy bearing down on his massive cock and almost squirting around him. Two orgasms in minutes, and there were many more still to come.

Finally, he withdrew from her, both of them breathing hard as his slick cock bobbed in the candlelight. Gabrielle looked over at Jack, who was in awe with wide eyes at what he was witnessing.

He motioned with his head and Gabrielle realized she hadn't even taken her panties off in the frenzy they had started. Standing up, she let her ass face her husband who was by now eagerly stroking his cock in the chair, and peeled down her panties slowly, bending over to show him her gaping wide pussy.

ou see how much he stretched me out?" Gabrielle asked him. All Jack could do was
d and keep jerking his dick while staring at her.

mbing back onto the bed, she turned over to face away from her lover, and Jordi
oped her ass cheeks with ease, sliding his tongue between them and moaning loudly.
en without warning his cock was inside her again, driven in with one hard thrust and
mming as deep as he could. With no warning, she came again and pressed her head
wn into the sheets below her. One thrust of him had made her cum with enough
udders to made her lightheaded.

vas like an unbelievable wave of ecstasy, making her body shudder again and again,
h high pitched wails coming from her throat that she'd never heard herself make
fore. Even though his cock was incredibly deep inside her, he was wielding it like a
tuoso, making sure he didn't hurt her and giving her just enough variety in his thrusts
keep her entire body on edge.

thout any resistance between his cock and her pussy the sensations were intense
tween them. It was as if searing heat was sending bolts of lightning through her
ssy. He didn't even need to touch her clit to make her cum repeatedly. Just the way
was fucking her steadily without stopping was enough.

gripped her hair and yanked it back, and she fiercely met his probing tongue with her
n as he moved with the last couple of inches of his cock as deep inside her as he
uld. Gabrielle knew he was probably getting close to finishing, and there was one
re desperate need she had. Looking over at Jack, she begged him for one more
ng.

vant him to cum inside me." She gasped. "I want to feel it. I want him to fill me up so
u can see it."

o it, babe. Let that big cock cum inside your pussy." Jack told her, his hand furiously
mping his cock. "I want to watch it. Take his cum."

di had stayed silent, just enjoying tugging on her long dark hair and squeezing her
s cheeks. When Gabrielle pulled off him and turned herself over, it was almost an
spoken signal between them. He was going to cum inside her pussy as deep as he
uld.

e spread her legs and Jordi grabbed one of her inner thighs, opening up her legs
en wider and it had the added advantage of allowing Jack to easily see his massive
k pushing back inside her. The angle and force of his first thrust made Gabrielle cry
again.

at's it…" Jack groaned. "Take that cock. Take his cum, baby. All of it."

expectedly, Jack stood up and approached the bed, still stroking his cock but
brielle reached a hand out to him, putting their fingers together and holding hands
an affectionate couple while her pussy was being plumbed from the other side. It

was perfect to feel his hand on hers while she watched her lover and her husband bo[?] ready to reach a climax.

"Oh, fuck…" Gabrielle said. "I can feel it. He's going to cum soon, baby." It was almos[?] as if Jordi wasn't even there, like the two of them were experiencing their own momer[?] even though another man was involved and in the room. Her lover kept fucking her deep and hard and Gabrielle watched him close his eyes, his massive thick cock swelling. She grabbed his cheek. "No. Jordi, look at me. Look into my eyes when you[?] cum."

A loud gasp and Jordi's eyes flew open, locking onto hers and his hips pushed into he[?] deep one more time. When the first blast erupted from his cock into her waiting tunne[?] Gabrielle could feel every pulse and ounce of warm heat driving inside her, making he[?] full and feeling like the most glorious sensation she'd ever had.

There seemed to be no end to the amount that was shooting out of him into her, and [?] the time he moved slowly inside her again, giving off little deep pants of satisfaction, s[?] could feel his white load flooding out of her onto the sheets below. Drip after thick drip[?] that confirmed what she had just done. Her husband was truly a cuckold and she was[?] truly a hotwife.

"Holy shit…" Jack gasped and then his cock exploded as well, the cum shooting out a[?] hitting Gabrielle on her naked chest, making her call out to him with a peal of satisfied[?] laughter. His cock dribbled a few more drops onto her chest, and then he stood back with a sigh, putting one knee on the bed.

Looking down between her legs, Gabrielle watched his eyes as Jordi finally withdrew long shaft that was coated with both of them. She looked into Jack's eyes and knew what she wanted him to see. Her lovers' cum inside her. Turning herself around, she knew that her sticky pussy was covered in Jordi's hot seed.

"He came so much, baby. He came inside my pussy. Can you see it?"

"I can see it all." Jack croaked. Gabrielle took him by the hand and then moved his ha[?] between her legs, feeling a delicious shiver of satisfaction when Jack dipped his fingertips between her legs and felt the sticky cum flowing out of her. Jordi sat back a[?] watched with a satisfied smile on his face.

Her husband played with the cum flowing out of her, and Gabrielle could feel his finge[?] tracing around her, his expression almost in awe. She knew what she had to ask, and[?] was something that would just make the entire experience come to an incredible conclusion. "Why don't you clean me up? Lick me. I want you to taste me."

Their eyes met. Without even hesitating, Jack moved down between her legs with his[?] head sliding up her inner thighs. Gabrielle almost stopped him. She hadn't intended f[?] him to clean her up with his mouth, but her husband seemed determined to fully entrench himself as a cuckold and taste her lover's cum straight from her pussy. His ngue moved up her thigh and then slid across her sticky pussy lips, starting to gently uch her in the sensitive areas that Jordi had just fucked. He was incredibly gentle, but e tip of his tongue collected some of the cum leaking out of her. Gabrielle couldn't lp but encourage him. "That's good, baby…clean me up. Get all that cum." When she roked his hair, he sighed like a child who was being given a reward.

felt so intimate and loving, like there wasn't even another man sitting there watching. hen she realized Jordi was still kneeling there on the bed, Gabrielle invited him over her, motioning that he should enjoy the moment together with them.

kissed her just as gently as Jack was gently cleaning her pussy, and he softly assaged her breasts while she enjoyed being tended to by her men. Both of them had lfilled what she was looking for perfectly.

hen Jack lifted his head from between her legs, he kissed her stomach and then laid s head on her as Jordi slid off the bed and stood up. He shook his head and almost oked sheepish at sharing such an intimate moment. "Thank you, Gabrielle. And Jack. at was something I will always remember." He nodded at both of them.

abrielle sighed. "We should thank you, Jordi." Jack just smiled up at her and kissed gher, finally nuzzling at her breasts. "But I think now we need to be alone. That was nazing."

rdi grabbed his clothing and left the room quietly, and suddenly the silence in the om was palpable. Gabrielle could hear them both breathing, and her body felt credibly relaxed. She'd gotten everything that she had wanted from both men.

nally, she realized she needed to clean herself up. "I should have a shower." Jack ed his head and smiled at her.

an I…wash you?" It was a brilliant suggestion. A way for them to reconnect intimately ter what had just happened in the bedroom. Gabrielle took his hand and led him wards their ensuite where he started the water and made the temperature perfect.

ne realized her legs were shaky and her while body was going to be sore in the orning, but for now, she enjoyed getting under the hot water naked with her husband. s soon as they were wet, Jack lovingly cleaned her entire body, beginning with rubbing r back and legs and then turning her around to kiss her while he cleaned her front. etween her legs, he took extra care to be gentle.

"hen she stepped out, her legs still shaky, he toweled her body off and then offered her me pyjamas, almost helping her into them. When Gabrielle finally slid into her bed, le kissed him gently. "Thank you."

Jo, thank you." Jack said. "Get some rest and we can talk in the morning."

Feeling grateful and lucky, Gabrielle slipped quickly into sleep, reliving the fantasy she had just experienced in her dreams as Jordi claimed her body over and over again. It was simply the beginning, that she knew, but it was going to be impossible to duplicate

EPILOGUE

Two days later they stood in the airport, waving Jordi through the security line. The night before had been filled with another passionate event, her young lover making her body experience such intensity that after they were finished Jack didn't even attempt to make love to her. He simply tucked her into bed. She was exhausted standing in the airport, but she also knew that the future of their sex life was something she was in firm control of from now on.

After the first time, Jack had made a point of taking her out for coffee and the two of them talked about more boundaries, how they both felt and some things they both fantasized about. It was incredible to have such an easy dialogue and be able to communicate her feelings about everything, plus have a partner who was excited about exploring even more with her.

After all, Jack had a business trip coming up and Gabrielle had a networking event to attend, where there would likely be a couple of eager men to flirt with. Perhaps even fool around with a bit if she so desired. The significant part about everything was that she could decide who and what she did.

She was melancholy when they arrived home after seeing Jordi leave their lives. The young man had changed a lot for their relationship, in a good way, of course, but that didn't mean that she wasn't going to miss her Spanish lover. And his massive equipment. Part of her goal was to find another man who was just as hung for her and Jack to enjoy.

Once they got home, he stole up to her from behind. "I have a surprise for you. Check your email." His hands wrapped around her waist and he kissed her neck.

Gabrielle grabbed her phone with a smile and saw that he'd reserved their trip. Except it wasn't for the place they had originally talked about. The resort claimed that it was an 'adults only' environment. She turned around and kissed him. "I'm so happy, babe. Thank you. What does adults only mean?"

Jack grinned. "Well, according to reviews, the place can be wild after hours. I thought maybe it was a good chance to dip our toes. And maybe make some new friends."

New friends. Did that mean swingers? Gabrielle's thoughts turned to videos she'd seen where a woman was being enjoyed by more than one man at the same time. Maybe that was something Jack wouldn't mind letting her indulge in. And, there were usually some pretty sexy women at resorts.

Now she just had to stay in shape. After all, there might be some fun to be had by the pool. Or elsewhere.

THE END

Thank you so much for reading and enjoying my writing! If you liked it, please leave a review _HERE_ on Amazon and help me reach more people with my work!

If you didn't like it, please give me feedback at _vickievaughanauthor@gmail.com_. I always welcome any and all viewpoints on my writing.

I self edit my books and also offer editing services to authors.

I also do commissions! If you would like a custom story written just for you, please check out my Fiverr profile _HERE_ to discuss it.

Join my mailing list at _www.vickievaughan.ca_ to receive promotions and free beta copies of upcoming works as well! Thanks again for your patronage!

Other titles now available:

The Butler Did Her – a steamy menage story!

I Love to Sweat – dual POV erotica!

Sharing The Bride – an Amazon #1 best seller!

Sharing the Bride 2: Cabin Fever

Sharing Her Husband – another Amazon #1 best seller!

Surrender and Submission

The Office Party

Dominating Her Husband

An Unexpected Seduction

The Athlete Bundle: 4 Erotic Stories

The White Hotwife Trilogy

Student House Submission: The Complete Series

Paradise Island

And Many More – Click _HERE_ for my Amazon author page!

Most titles free to read on Kindle Unlimited!

Printed in Great Britain
by Amazon

45699000R00046